Murder Is Elementary
(A Susan Wiles Schoolhouse Mystery)

by

Diane Weiner

Copyright 2014 by Diane Weiner

For information, email **Cozy Cat Press**, cozycatpress@aol.com or visit our website at: www.cozycatpress.com

COZY CAT
PRESS

ISBN: 978-1-939816-37-5

Printed in the United States of America

Cover design by Katherine Janda
http://tea-and-jellybeans.tumblr.com

1 2 3 4 5 6 7 8 9 10

This book is dedicated to my husband, Robert, and my children—Allison, Kevin, Eric, and Laura—for all their help, enthusiasm, and support.

Chapter 1

Susan Wiles scanned the audience—parents videotaping with their smart phones, angelic grandparents, restless siblings, weary teachers. Before retirement, Susan had always loved being in charge of the annual holiday concert. She was proud to have had her elementary chorus singing in two part harmony. With this new music teacher, they were singing tired and true Christmas carols, all in unison. They weren't even making any dynamic contrasts or carrying the phrases through to the end of the bars. *The Twelve Days of Christmas*, really? Show some originality.

Susan remembered how the anticipation of winter break had always made her feel as if popcorn kernels were bursting under her skin. Now she felt like vanilla frosting—yes, it was sweet to be retired but honestly, how much vanilla frosting could you eat at one sitting? Whenever she hinted at missing work, her husband Mike quickly reminded her of the rehearsals which often spanned the dinner hour, the frayed bowties and vests that the school couldn't afford to replace, and…the technology. When did accompanying a chorus on a Wurlitzer console give way to hooking up an ipod to a sound system?

Susan wiped her wire-rimmed glasses—no, her wire-rimmed *bifocals*—on her skirt and readjusted them on her nose. The bifocals really irked her. She was, after all, in great health (except for the extra 20 pounds she carried despite daily walks and a Dr. Oz approved diet). And she wasn't about to give in to gray hair. No, siree.

Monthly salon visits were right up there with grocery shopping and paying bills. Her blue gray eyes betrayed her though. That's where she felt her age. Bifocals? Really?

Susan and Mike rose from their uncomfortable metal folding chairs. Much of the audience hurried toward the back of the cafeteria where parent volunteers were conducting a bake sale.

"So, you couldn't stay away," chided fifth grade teacher Antonio Petrocelli. His dimples were showing. Antonio was one of Susan's former coworker.

"I know you, you had to come and check up on the new music teacher," said Antonio. His wife Hayley approached, balancing a plate of Christmas cookies and a coffee. "So, is she driving you crazy with all that free time on her hands?" asked Antonio, turning his attention to Mike.

Mike replied, "What do you mean? I actually love having the spices alphabetized and the towels sorted by size and color."

Susan swatted him on the shoulder, feeling a little hurt. "I've been using my time very productively. You know you love having the house organized," answered Susan. She'd never admit it, but she couldn't help wondering what her next project would be—polishing the silver? Bleaching her scuffed Reeboks?

Her thoughts were interrupted by the inevitable feedback from the microphone on the stage. Amidst the buzz in the cafeteria, the assistant principal called the audience back to their seats. Susan knew what would follow. Vicky Rogers was about to take the stage and give her usual speech—how AWESOME the chorus was, how AWESOME the parents were for supporting their children, how AWESOME the music teacher was, and how PROUD she was to be principal of Westbrook Elementary. Like a ceiling fan winding down, the audience gradually quieted. When Mrs. Rogers didn't immediately appear, Susan noticed Mr. Ford, the assistant principal, beginning to clumsily improvise. *He's trying to buy some time*, thought Susan. *It looks like he could use a bit of help.* Susan approached the stage and whispered in Mr. Ford's ear that she'd go find Vicky. She had remembered seeing her head toward her office. Susan hurried down the hall, pushed open the heavy glass door to the administrative suite, and passed the secretary's desk en route to the principal's office. She knocked. She knocked again. Then she turned the knob, opened the door, and screamed.

Chapter 2

A half- eaten funfetti cupcake sat on top of the heavy oak desk, surrounded by a legal pad, family photos, a laptop, and an agenda book. Behind the desk, next to the rolling chair, Vicky Rogers was a motionless lump in a tweed suit. Audience members began storming the office.

"Someone call 911."

"What happened?"

"Is she dead?"

Mike, Hayley, and Antonio had been sitting near the cafeteria exit and were amongst the first to reach Vicky's office after hearing the horrific scream. Mr. Ford arrived shortly behind them, yelling to the school social worker to keep people away. Mike, his volunteer fireman experience kicking in, bent over Vicky, listening for breathing and checking for a pulse.

"I think she's gone," said Mike. "Maybe it was a heart attack."

Within minutes, the paramedics arrived followed by two detectives. Luckily, the roads were clear that night and nowhere was very far from anywhere else in the small town of Westbrook. Susan noticed that the tiny office seemed not to have been disturbed. There was no blood, no weapon in sight. The paramedics turned Vicky onto her back and listened for a heartbeat. Susan was amazed by the effort the paramedics were putting into reviving an obviously dead body. She watched as they injected Vicky with what she assumed was epinephrine (she'd seen that done a thousand times on the television crime shows she loved to watch). They started chest compressions and then shocked Susan's former boss several times with a defibrillator. Susan couldn't help thinking about how satisfying this scene would be to many of the employees at Westbrook. Susan had always gotten along well with Vicky but not everyone did. Eventually the paramedics confirmed that Vicky was indeed dead.

Jackson Simpson, a paunchy young detective with sparse brown hair, began shooing people out of the hallway. Susan knew him well. He took his job very seriously—so seriously that he went ballistic when his partner Lynette discussed "hypothetical" cases with her newly retired, overly imaginative mom, Susan. He began asking the onlookers what they'd witnessed. Lynette was there now too, assessing the scene.

"Everyone out," ordered Lynette. "That means you too, Mom." Susan hated when Lynette glared at her with those deep chestnut eyes.

Susan took her time leaving the scene, soaking in all the details as she exited the office. A broken vase caught her eye. The vase was normally kept on the conference table. Susan remembered that from her working days. Vicky had always kept fresh flowers on the table. Whenever they'd had team leader meetings someone would make a comment about tax payer money being spent on beautifying Vicky's personal space. Of course, those comments were always made out of Vicky's earshot. There was no way that Vicky, sitting at her desk, would have accidentally knocked over the vase since it would have been across the room.

Jackson took photos as Lynette bagged the cupcake, laptop, and various small items that might be useful in determining cause of death. Susan saw Lynette inspecting a large, freshly minted bruise on Vicky's right cheek. Then she watched as Lynette inspected the rest of Vicky's face. Even from her vantage point, Susan could see that Vicky's lips were a bit swollen. Someone must have hit her in the face, thought Susan. Was that the cause of death?

Lynette bent down and picked up pieces of the broken vase. "This is looking like murder," said Lynette. She was talking to Jackson but Susan couldn't help overhearing, since she was about two inches outside of Vicky's office at this point. Lynette had told her to get out of the office but she didn't say how far she had to go.

"Do we have any contact information?" asked Jackson. "We'll need to notify the next of kin." Susan saw Lynette look around the desk, probably for a purse or a cell phone, but neither materialized.

"She has a husband, Javier, and a teen age daughter, Carolina," answered Susan, poking her head into the doorway.

"Mom, I told you to leave," said Lynette.

"You know, Lynette, if it weren't for me introducing you to Nancy Drew books when you were ten, you probably wouldn't have even gone into law enforcement. Let me help. Vicky's mother died a few years ago, and her dad's in a nursing home in Florida." Susan's stomach knotted at the sudden thought of Vicky's teenage daughter, Carolina, hearing this news. Carolina had been one of Susan's favorite students and although she was now in high-school, they were still close. Susan had met Javier once at a faculty party but only that once. She scrolled through her contacts list and jotted down Vicky's address and home phone number. Then she handed it to Jackson.

"Let's go home," said Mike, putting his arm around Susan. "It's been a long night." Susan couldn't have agreed more.

Chapter 3

Carolina, dressed in a matronly black a-line dress accessorized with a single strand of pearls, looked like a little girl playing dress up in her mother's high heeled shoes. Susan and Mike gave her a hug. At 16, Carolina was being forced prematurely into maturity. Her dad Javier, barely an inch taller and with the same jet black hair and olive skin, stood next to her in the alcove of the funeral home, greeting a procession of Vicky's friends, colleagues, and acquaintances. Susan noticed that his blue dress shirt was wrinkled under his black suit. His eyes were red and moist, and his breath smelled vaguely of alcohol. The funeral hall buzzed with hushed condolences.

"Sorry for your loss,"

"How tragic."

"She was so young."

"We all loved Vicky."

Hayley and Antonio were next in line.

"Let us know if there's anything we can do," said Hayley.

"I'm really going to miss her," said Antonio. Susan knew he meant it. Antonio was an aspiring principal. His charm, confidence, and dramatic flair allowed his colleagues to easily envision him in that role.

"Are you going to step in and help Mr. Ford?" asked Susan. Vicky had often allowed Antonio to handle issues with angry parents and misbehaving students. In fact, he was mistaken for the assistant principal on more than one occasion.

"I certainly will do anything I can to keep the school up and running," said Antonio. "I'm thankful that Vicky allowed me to have so much administrative experience these past few years."

That's Antonio, thought Susan. Always politically correct. From Susan's perspective, Vicky had appeared to be grooming Antonio for the next opening in their small school district—an opening that was likely to occur only upon the death or retirement of an incumbent. Westbrook was the kind of town where people didn't voluntarily leave. It offered a small town, wholesome lifestyle which in modern times was increasingly difficult to find.

"I'm sure he'll miss her in many ways," said Hayley.

Susan thought she detected a hint of sarcasm in her voice.

Next in line were Theresa Rizzo and Jody Decker. Theresa taught fourth grade at Westbrook Elementary. Barely five foot two, she was Italian through and through with her wavy dark hair and brown eyes. Theresa had often talked about how much she'd enjoyed growing up in a large family. She was one of eight children, all of whom still lived in Westbrook. She shook Javier's hand and introduced herself.

"Vicky gave me my first job. I'll never forget her," said Theresa.

Jody Decker was the school social worker. She was tall with reddish brown hair and a hefty build. Her hands dwarfed Carolina's as she clasped them and said, "I'm here for you." Jody was new to Westbrook. The funeral home echoed with condolences.

"My son loved Miss Vicky."

"How will the school go on without her?"

"She *was* Westbrook Elementary."

Many parents expressed their condolences, however some were conspicuously absent. Susan noticed that

Blaze Conrad wasn't there mourning or offering condolences. *In fact*, thought Susan, *Blaze Conrad certainly had motive to kill Vicky*. His son Ryan had allegedly been molested by his teacher. Blaze was convinced that Vicky was aware of this but swept it under the rug, with the help of Antonio Petrocelli. The murmurs continued as people began to leave the building.

"She looks so peaceful."

"We'll be praying for your family."

"She's with God now."

It was already dark outside when Javier and Carolina left the funeral parlor. Susan and Mike followed them out to the parking lot. Susan wiped her moist eyes as she imagined Javier and Carolina going home to a cold and empty house.

Chapter 4

The Petracelli household was already awake when the sun came up several days after the murder. "Hurry up and brush your teeth, Tony," said Hayley.

Tony could be a child model—he was that adorable. It wasn't just Hayley who thought so either. Everywhere she took him, people would comment on his thick sandy-colored hair and sparkly blue eyes. Then they'd suggest that she get him into modeling or commercials. Once a woman in the grocery store even handed Hayley her business card. She was a casting agent for an advertising agency. Hayley thought about contacting her but then she got pregnant...and sick....and exhausted....

"You and Daddy have to leave in a few minutes," said Hayley. The sun coming in through the blinds left slats of sunlight on the kitchen table.

"I need to be there extra early," said Antonio. It was the last day before winter break. Antonio had been helping Mr. Ford run the school since Vicky's death.

"Good thing the week before winter break is mostly arts and crafts, parties, and holiday videos. My class doesn't even realize they have a sub," said Antonio.

"I'm sure they miss you," said Hayley

In spite of the unfortunate circumstances, Hayley knew Antonio was enjoying his new role. Good thing he enjoyed it because he'd need a promotion in order to keep up with the payments on their dream house and now a new baby. Hayley was used to a certain lifestyle and she knew Antonio didn't mind it either. Their lifestyle was so superior to what he'd grown up with. Antonio once told her that his mother fed him Kraft Macaroni and Cheese almost every night because it was all she could afford.

"Have a good day," said Hayley.

"Don't forget your lunchbox," she called to Tony. "I made some of those M&M brownies for dessert. I gave you some too, Hun."

"Thanks," said Antonio. "See you around dinner time." He gave her a quick kiss and shepherded Tony out the door.

"Don't forget to lock the door," Hayley called after him. *He definitely needed to remember to lock the door,* she thought. He should have locked the bedroom door that day when he thought I was visiting my parents, thought Hayley. She felt her cheeks turning red.

Hayley took a bottle of formula out of the refrigerator. She knew the baby would be waking up hungry any time now. She was right. When he started crying, she went upstairs, changed his diaper, and brought him downstairs for breakfast. As she was strapping him into his high chair, the phone rang. It was her mother.

"Hi, mom. What's up?" Hayley fed the baby with one hand while holding the phone with the other.

"I just wanted to say hello and see what time you wanted us over on Christmas Eve. I can't wait to give Tony his presents. He's going to love the iPad we got him. I also picked up a radio-controlled car at *Toys R Us* the other day. I bought the baby a few shares of Apple stock. "

"You're going to spoil Tony, Mom. He'll be asking for a Lamborghini by the time he's 16."

Hayley's mother was pedigreed all the way and spent her days getting manicures, playing tennis (racket ball in the winter), and lunching with the ladies at the country club. She'd never worked a day in her life.

"Why shouldn't I give him the things his *father* can't afford to get him?"

Hayley hated the tone her Mom used whenever she referred to Antonio. Antonio had worked hard at convincing Hayley's parents that a theater major with a financial need scholarship would be a worthy partner for their only child. When the acting thing didn't pan out, Antonio became a teacher. That was an even harder sell. At least with acting there was a remote possibility of becoming the next Brad Pitt.

"I was thinking around 7:00. Antonio is going to make linguine with clam sauce."

"Does Tony eat that?" said her mom.

"No, but I'll make him some pasta with butter," said Hayley. "Come by around 7:00."

"Did they offer Antonio the principal job yet?" With prodding from both Hayley and his in-laws, Antonio had decided a few years ago to pursue administration and the larger salary that came with it.

"Not yet, but I'm sure they will," said Hayley.

"Let's hope so. I'll see you soon."

"See you soon," said Hayley.

Chapter 5

Antonio walked Tony to 'before school' care in the cafeteria and then headed to his office. For now, it was his temporary office but he hoped that after Christmas it might become permanent. They'd need to fill the position soon and Lord knows he was still available. His eyes narrowed and his jaw tightened. He should already be a principal. There'd been an opening in a neighboring school just before Thanksgiving. The principal, dealing with a sudden health crisis, had decided to take early retirement. Dear sweet Vicky, his friend and mentor, refused to recommend him for the position. That b… laughed in his face when he asked her about it.

"Antonio, Antonio, Antonio. What makes you think you could possibly handle that job? You lack not only the expertise, but the professionalism and ethical compass needed to be a principal."

Antonio felt his shoulders tensing. Perhaps he'd crossed some ethical lines with Vicky but wasn't he just following her example? Antonio's dark thoughts stood in contrast to the cheerful holiday decorations lining the path to his office. Reindeer, wreaths, *Feliz Navidad* written on a Christmas bell, and, of course, the obligatory menorah. With each step he felt as if he were being mocked.

"Good morning, Mr. Petrocelli," said Sandra from behind her desk. Sandra dressed like a school marm and her permed hairstyle dated back to the 80's.

"Good morning, Sandra. Are you okay? You seem a little preoccupied."

"I'm still a little shaken about having been questioned by the police. They asked me all about the day of the murder. The detectives wanted to know who'd come by the office to see Vicky that day and who I thought might want to kill Vicky."

"What did you tell them?" said Antonio

"I said I could think of plenty of people who'd threatened to kill Vicky over the years. I told them about Blaze Conrad—that was an obvious choice. Then there were the Moores."

"The Moores, oh yeah, I remember them," said Antonio.

"They were concerned about their daughter being bullied by the kids in her class. Vicky told them it was their own fault for raising a child with low self esteem. She told them if they'd taught her to be self confident she wouldn't be such an easy target," said Sandra.

"Mr. Moore went ballistic and threatened to kill her, right?"

"Yes, but he was angry. Who would blame him? That didn't mean he'd actually plan a murder," said Sandra.

"They wound up pulling their daughter out of Westbrook and putting her in a charter school. That was a civil way to handle the situation. Where's Mr. Ford?"

"Mr. Ford's at a meeting. He'll be back around lunch time. There are several phone calls to return. Mr. Ford said to give you these." Sandra handed Antonio an array of yellow message slips. She was sweeter than apple pie and competent to the max.

Antonio poured himself a cup of coffee. He had previously taken his coffee with cream and sugar but since becoming an interim principal, he started drinking it black. It was still a little early to return phone calls so he began answering emails. Jody Decker, the social worker, came in with a stack of paperwork for him to sign. She was wearing a black skirt, a gray sweater, and unusually high heels for the workplace. He'd heard the tapping of heels on the linoleum warning him that she was coming. Jody was meticulous at her job and pleasant for the most part, but her voice reminded him of the sound the garbage disposal made when chewing up egg shells and coffee grinds.

"I walked by Vicky's office and it seemed surreal. I still feel her sitting there, talking on the phone or typing on the computer," said Jody.

"I know," said Antonio, "It seems like she's still here." Antonio wanted to add, "Like a ghost haunting the castle," but he stopped himself.

"So the police think it was murder?" Jody readjusted her headband.

"That's what I hear." Antonio flipped through the papers Jody had brought him.

"Do they have any clues as to who did it?"

"Not that I know of," replied Antonio.

"I'll bet dollars to donuts it was Blaze Conrad." Jody waved her index finger. "Remember how angry he was when Vicky was exonerated? He even said to that TV reporter that he could kill her for covering up what was happening to his son."

"Lot's of people say things like that when they're angry." He signed the packet in the places Jody had marked with a mini sticky note.

"Yes, but we know he had a violent streak. Remember how he keyed her car right in broad daylight? With witnesses right there in the parking lot?"

"I'm sure the police are looking into it." Antonio handed the documents back to Jody. "I really need to get back to work. Have a good break if I don't see you."

Antonio worked for a few hours. Mr. Ford returned around noon bearing hot pizza. Snow flurries had melted on his hat and trench coat. Antonio and the office staff were invited into his office for lunch. It was a nice prelude to Christmas break.

Chapter 6

It still seemed a little strange, being home on a weekday morning. Johann nuzzled against Susan as she poured Meow Mix into his bowl. He liked rubbing against her well-worn sweatpants, which were almost, but not quite, as soft as his shiny black fur. Ludwig, the gray tabby, immediately started eating. Susan heard a knock at the door. She was grateful that her cats didn't go crazy and bark like maniacs the way dogs did when someone knocked. Susan was definitely a cat person.

"Just a minute." She padded to the door in her fuzzy slippers. Spending the entire day in slippers was one of the perks of retirement. She peered through the peephole (not so easy with those bifocals) and saw Carolina.

"Hey, honey, come on in," said Susan "Let me take your jacket."

"Thanks." Carolina was crying as she stepped into the foyer and shook the snow off of her boots. Susan noticed that Carolina had lost a few pounds.

"How about some hot chocolate?" Susan didn't wait for a response. She hugged Carolina, and then she padded back into the kitchen where she filled up the tea kettle. "How are you holding up?"

"Not so great. I keep hearing her voice inside my head and smelling her perfume. Sometimes I'm just sad, other times I'm angry. Furious is more like it. Last night I just started throwing things around the living room. I must have thrown every book we own out of the bookshelf. I want whoever killed my mom to spend the rest of his life locked away in prison, or better yet dead. Too bad we no longer have the death penalty here."

"I'm going to make sure we catch that person Carolina. We have Lynette on our side. She's a great detective."

"I know I can depend on you. I miss Mom so much and not only that, I'm afraid I'm going to lose my dad too."

"You're dad will still be here for you."

"No, Mrs. W. There are things you don't know about my dad."

"What do you mean? What kinds of things?"

"I have no one else to confide in. You have to help me."

"Of course, I will. What sorts of things?" Susan poured packets of hot chocolate into mugs. No matter how carefully she poured the packet into the cup, cocoa powder always wound up on the counter.

"Well, my dad...he drank a lot. He and my mom fought about it all the time. Sometimes he got violent. He once gave her a black eye. No one can know. She would have been so embarrassed if anyone knew. He lost his job a few weeks ago and got even worse. My mom kicked him out. He's been living in an apartment, which my mom was paying for. He begged to stay but my mom had had it. She even saw a divorce lawyer."

"I'm so sorry, sweetie. What can I do to help?" Susan poured water into the mugs. Then she reached behind the quinoa for the bag of Mint Milanos.

"I need to know if my dad had anything to do with my Mom's murder. I need you to help me find out before the police find out about him. If he is involved, I want to know first. If he isn't the killer, then I want to know who is. Maybe then I'll be able to start pulling my life back together."

"Do you really think your Dad could possibly be involved? Getting physical after drinking is one thing but murder is quite a stretch."

"I never would have been able to picture it but lately...he's changed so much." Carolina began sobbing. Susan handed her a tissue.

"Do you want me to talk to Lynette?"

"No, please don't. Just help me snoop around a bit and see if there's anything tying him into the murder. I don't want to find out he's guilty on the five o'clock news. If he was involved, I want to know first so I can digest it."

"I'm certainly no Kinsey Malone, but I'll do what I can."

"He bowls on Saturday mornings. Let's go to his apartment while he's out. He gave me a key." She pulled the key out of her pocket to show Susan.

"Okay, it's a date." Susan couldn't say no to Carolina but wondered what can of worms they might be about to open.

Chapter 7

While Susan was digesting what Carolina had just told her, Lynette and Jackson were at the station discussing the bruises found on Vicky's face. Not knowing about Javier's history of violence, they focused instead on Blaze Conrad.

"These bruises don't look that severe. I'm not sure these were the cause of death," said Lynette.

"Remember last year? We found that old lady dead in her apartment with bruises just like this. Her nurse had been beating her and that caused her death. Looks really similar," said Jackson.

"Your flawless memory hidden under that goofy veneer still surprises me," said Lynette. "I guess you're right. The medical examiner has ruled out heart attack or embolism. We have to wait till he finishes the lab work but for now it seems like the most plausible explanation. Let's head over to the school and interview some of the faculty. Meanwhile, I have one of the deputies checking into the information we got from the secretary this morning."

Jackson opened the passenger door for Lynette and slid behind the wheel.

"The students should be out by now," said Lynette. Westbrook Elementary was a sturdy, one story building complete with a flag pole out front. The brick exterior weathered well and the school looked as new as the day it was built. There was a circular drive in front which the buses used. On the left side of the school there was a small parking lot and a drive through street where the parents dropped off and picked up their children. On the other side of the school, there was a large parking lot used by faculty and visitors. A few spots nearest the front of the school were reserved for administration and VIP visitors.

"This school looks exactly as it did when I went here," said Lynette.

"This is how I remember it too," said Jackson. "It's amazing that after all these years, the population has remained steady. They haven't needed to add on like so many of the schools near here. My niece actually goes to school in a trailer believe it or not. They call it a portable classroom. She says it gets pretty darn cold during the winter months. I bought her a fleece hoodie last Christmas to wear inside her classroom."

When they entered the school, Sandra had already set up a conference room and called in the teachers who Jackson and Lynette wanted to speak with. Theresa Rizzo came in first. She wore a teal-colored sweater. Lynette noticed that it really flattered her skin tone.

"Have a seat, Miss Rizzo," said Jackson. "We're interviewing people who were at the concert the night of the murder or who may have had contact with Mrs. Rogers during the day."

"Well, I was at the holiday concert. I was there with my friend Jody. When Mrs. Wiles screamed, we were amongst the first to reach the office. Mr. Ford asked Jody and me to keep bystanders from entering the office. When Mrs. Wiles screamed, most of the audience got up and headed in her direction."

"What was your relationship like with Mrs. Rogers?" said Lynette

"She has always been nice to me. I was a brand new teacher when I applied here. Vicky was supportive. She asked what supplies I needed for my room and got me everything I requested. When one of my parents called her to complain about something that happened with their child, she refused to discuss it with them until they talked to me first."

"Can you think of anyone who may have wanted to harm Vicky?" asked Jackson.

"Not really. Not everyone loved her all the time but I can't think of anyone around here who would have hated her enough to kill her."

"Thank you, Miss Rizzo. We'll be in touch if we have further questions." Jackson stood up and opened the door for her.

He watched her walk out of the office suite.

"Ask her out," said Lynette. I saw how you were looking at her."

"I don't even know if she's in a relationship," said Jackson. "You know I have a terrible record when it comes to relationships."

"It's because you act like a bumbling keystone cop. You have to stop hiding behind your goofiness and let people see the real Jackson. You're a grown up now. You're not still competing with your Mensa member brother for your parent's attention." Lynette knew that Jackson yearned to be married and start a family. He was in his late thirties and had confided this to her.

"You're a diamond in the rough, Jackson. It's time to start polishing."

"Can you ask your mom if she knows whether or not Theresa Rizzo is seeing someone?" said Jackson.

"What are you, a teenager? I'll ask, but my mom hasn't worked here since last year so I doubt she'll know." Just then Sandra poked her head in the doorway.

"Miss Decker is here," said Sandra.

"Thanks," said Lynette. "We're ready for her."

Sandra escorted the social worker into the conference room.

"Thanks for coming by, Ms. Decker. I know it's the end of the day and you're probably ready to get out of here." Lynette pulled a chair out from the conference table and Jody sat down.

"No problem. I want to help in any way possible," said Jody.

"Can you tell us about the night Vicky Rogers died?" asked Lynette.

"Well, it was the night of the holiday concert, as you know. During intermission there was a bake sale run by the parents in the back of the cafeteria. I was with my friend Theresa. We bought coffee and chocolate chip cookies and chatted with our friends. The cafeteria was packed. When it was time for the concert to resume, we returned to our seats. We were expecting Mrs. Rogers to say a few words but she seemed to have disappeared. Then we heard a scream. Jody and I flew out of our seats and raced down the corridor. That's when we realized something had happened to Mrs. Rogers. Mr. Ford asked us to help him keep people out of the office."

"Can you tell us anything about Mrs. Rogers that might be useful to our investigation?" asked Jackson.

"Well," said Jody, "Vicky had a mean streak. There was this teacher—Miss Green—that she had it in for. Vicky had told her to teach math in the morning but Miss Green argued that she preferred teaching reading in the morning and math in the afternoon. I doubt Vicky really cared, but because Miss Green challenged her, she got vindictive. When we were making the class lists at the beginning of the school year she loaded her up with every behavior problem in fifth grade."

"So in your opinion, there may have been people here who were angry enough to kill her?" asked Jackson.

"I'd have to say yes. Some loved her but there were more who hated her."

"Thanks, Miss Decker. You've been very helpful. Give us a call if you think of anything else," said Lynette.

"I certainly will," said Jody.

Next, Sandra brought in the head custodian. He was tall and lanky, probably about Vicky's age. Lynette and Jackson introduced themselves.

"Hello, Mr. Abrams. We're investigating Mrs. Roger's murder. Thanks for coming in," said Jackson.

"No problem. I hope I can help."

"I see here that you grew up with Vicky Rogers," said Jackson, as he rifled through his notes.

"Yes. My family lived next door to her up in Ithaca. We used to have frequent barbecues together during the summer months. Her family had a pool. We had an open invitation to come over and swim. Vicky and I used to ride our bikes to school together. When the head custodian position opened up, Vicky was nice enough to call me. She knew I had recently lost my job."

"What was she was like growing up," asked Lynette.

"She was a lot of fun, and a bit of a daredevil. She was also really stubborn. She was always fighting with her mother about something or other. I remember when she got her first car. Her parents had bought her a used Toyota for her birthday. I'd have been ecstatic to receive a car as a birthday gift but not Vicky. She kicked and screamed about it not being a brand new car. Vicky took the keys, slid in, and crashed it deliberately into their family car which was parked in the driveway. She destroyed both cars but she didn't care. She had to have her way. She had her father wrapped around her little finger but her mom was onto her."

"That's very interesting. Thank you for your help, Mr. Abrams," said Lynette.

"By the way, did you happen to see anything unusual the night of the murder?"

"Hmm, let me think. It's probably nothing."

"It's been our experience that sometimes the smallest details help solve the case," said Lynette.

"It's just that I know I turned out the lights after I cleaned the office," said Mr. Abrams. "I was outside sweeping the front walk during the concert and I saw the overhead light turn on in Vicky's office through the window. She never used the overhead light—said the fluorescents gave her a headache. She always used the lamp on her desk. It struck me as odd."

"Did you see anyone in the office?" asked Jackson.

"I can't say I did, but I was mopping floors most of that night. Two of my crew called in sick so I had to cover and help Ivy clean the rooms. God forbid the district would spend the money to send in subs to help us."

"It always comes down to money, doesn't it?" chuckled Jackson. "Thank you for your time. We may be in touch again."

After Mr. Abrams left, Lynette turned to Jackson. "What's our next move?" Jackson checked his phone. "I've got the address for Blaze Conrad. Why don't we follow up on that? I'll send a car to Mr. Conrad's home to pick him up. It won't take long to get him down to the station," said Jackson.

Chapter 8

While Jackson was calling the station, Lynette's phone vibrated. It was her Mom.

"Mom, what is it? You know I'm at work."

"Yes, I know, but I was wondering how the Vicky Roger's murder case is coming along. I was thinking, maybe you should look into that parent, Blaze Conrad. I happened to be in Vicky's office one day last year and heard him arguing with Vicky. He was really irate. I even heard him threaten to kill Vicky."

"Stay out of this, Mom. I know how to do my job. How's that quilt progressing?"

"Okay, I can take a hint. And the quilt is coming along just fabulously. Talk to you soon."

Lynette put away her phone and exited the school with Jackson. They got into the cruiser and started toward the station. Lynette turned to Jackson.

"So, when are you going to ask Theresa Rizzo out on a date?" asked Lynette

"Oh, I don't even know if she's available." Jackson blushed.

"Come on, Jackson. You *are* a detective aren't you? You don't even have to be a detective to figure out that; you just need to check out social media." She grabbed her phone, and typed in some information. "See; right on her home page it says she's single. *Single.* You need to go for it before someone else snatches her up. "

"What should I say?"

"Ask her what kind of movies she likes and then casually mention that you could pick her up and go see something together."

"I don't know…I'll have to think about it."

"Man up, partner. Go after what you want. She seems really nice."

They arrived at the station and waited for Blaze Conrad. Jackson straightened the papers on his desk into a neat pile and grabbed a bag of barbeque-flavored chips from a drawer.

"Here, have some." He ripped open the bag and offered some to Lynette. Within minutes the phone rang.

"This is Officer Reynolds. I have Mr. Conrad here."

"Thanks, we'll be right there," said Lynette. She grabbed a yellow legal pad and a pen. Jackson grabbed the portable voice recorder. Lynette and Jackson headed to the interrogation room which was cold and uncomfortable. The temperature was deliberately turned down to keep the suspects on edge. Lynette always wore her sweater. The walls were gray cinder block and the furniture was metal—*bed pan metal,* as Jackson always referred to it. The tile floor and bare walls amplified every sound.

Blaze Conrad was dressed in jeans and a denim shirt. He'd taken off his coat but put it right back on. Lynette thought his fingers looked blue. Blaze removed his knit cap and smoothed his strawberry blond hair.

"Thank you for coming in voluntarily," said Lynette. "We're hoping you can help with our investigation." She turned on the voice recorder.

"Mr. Conrad, how long had you known Vicky Rogers?"

"Since my son started kindergarten. I'd say two years."

"Can you describe your relationship with her?" asked Lynette.

"I think she was a snake and had no business being a principal. She was oblivious to what went on at that school and had no empathy for the students." Blaze opened and closed his weathered fists.

"Why do you say that?" asked Lynette.

"She's supposed to protect her students. My son showed every sign in the book that he was being molested. My wife and I—or should I say my *ex-wife* and I—came to Mrs. Rogers for help but she did nothing. If she did believe us, she just swept it under the rug. If that teacher hadn't been caught in the act, who knows how long my son would have continued to suffer."

"That's terrible. I know that had to have been very upsetting," said Lynette.

Jackson chimed in.

"So, Mr. Conrad, where were you the night Vicky Rogers was killed?" Jackson's serious tone was off set by the fact that he was chomping on potato chips.

"I was at the dollar movies. Alone." The metal chair clanked as Blaze Conrad pushed back from the table.

"And what time was that?" asked Jackson. He licked orange salt off his fingers as he waited for a response. Lynette thought that if Jackson was trying to play *bad cop,* he should have lost the bag of chips. The finger licking simply wasn't enhancing the tough guy image.

"I dunno. I guess I got there around 7:30. I watched the James Bond movie. I was home by 10:00 cause I remember turning on the early news."

"Did anyone see you there?" asked Jackson.

"Like I said, I was alone. Ryan stays at his mom's during the week. I don't like him seeing violence so I decided not to go see it on the weekend."

"Did you happen to see Vicky Rogers that night, Mr. Conrad?" asked Jackson. "Did you threaten to kill her or in any way have anything to do with her death?" Jackson rose slightly from his seat, pounded his fist on the desk, and put his face closer to Blaze like the cops on TV did when they were trying to be intimidating. Lynette thought he was about as intimidating as a Muppet.

"It's no secret I hated her. She knew exactly what was going on between that sick bastard of a teacher and my son but did absolutely nothing. We had a conference with her, my wife and me. Ryan was not right. He used to love school but suddenly cried when we dropped him off. He also started wetting the bed. Mrs. Rogers told us she'd look into it. Acted all sympathetic and everything. If that other teacher hadn't walked in on them it may have still been going on." Blaze was practically shouting.

"If that were my child," said Lynette, I would have ripped her apart like a mother tiger." She twisted her hands for emphasis. "I wouldn't blame you for going after her. It would make me angry enough to kill. Did you kill her, Mr. Conrad?"

"Of course not. I won't lie and say I wasn't happy that she got what she deserved, but I had nothing to do with it." He readjusted his jacket and sat forward in his seat.

"Okay, Mr. Conrad. We'll check out your alibi. You are free to go. Thanks for your cooperation," said Lynette.

Chapter 9

Susan awoke at precisely 7:06 am. She never had to set an alarm clock. It was uncanny how she woke up between seven and seven fifteen virtually every morning. She had imagined she'd sleep later once she retired but her internal clock was too firmly set. Mike was snoring loudly beside her in the four poster bed. It was a wonder she could sleep at all. On a good day he sounded like the suction machine the dentist used. On a bad one he sounded more like a lawnmower. Mike was a night owl. Just about the time Susan was falling asleep on the couch watching *Law and Order*, Mike was jumping on the stationary bike or catching up on *Words with Friends*. Susan took a quick shower and pulled on her favorite jeans and a cable knit sweater. Then she headed downstairs for breakfast.

Let's see, thought Susan, *oatmeal or oatmeal?* She chose oatmeal. Ludwig nuzzled against her leg as she ate and read the paper. She tore out the crossword puzzle to do later. After her second cup of coffee, Susan carried the mug and bowl into the kitchen and rinsed them in the sink. She would load the dishwasher later. She put on her Reeboks, grabbed her keys, and drove to Carolina's.

When she arrived in Carolina's driveway, Susan honked the horn. She knew that texting, "I'm here" was the cooler thing to do but it would take her longer to do that than to get out of the car and ring the bell. Carolina came out of the house wearing a down jacket and a red scarf with matching mittens.

"I'm so glad to see you. I'm so anxious to find some information today. Thanks for doing this." Carolina slid into the seat beside her. Susan softened the radio. In the rear view mirror, Susan saw a car that had been parked down the street start up. It was driving slowly, keeping its distance from Susan's Prius.

"You'll have to give me directions," said Susan. *That car is still following me*, thought Susan. She didn't want to alarm Carolina so she didn't say anything.

"Go to the light and turn right. Then keep going. Make another right at the four way stop."

After Susan made the turn, she no longer saw the mysterious car. It was probably just her overactive imagination.

Ten minutes later, they pulled into the parking lot of the Apple Tree Apartment Complex. It was an older complex but the exterior appeared freshly painted and the grounds were well maintained from what she could see.

Carolina used her key to open the door of her dad's apartment. The musty smell of dry heat greeted them. The apartment was tiny and looked as though it had been furnished in the eighties. The walls were covered in cream-colored wall paper with a tan-textured print that could have been leaves or maybe even feathers. The wall behind the sofa was paneled with cherry-colored wood. The gold-toned shag carpeting was well worn. Despite the midmorning sun, the living room was dark and gloomy. There was a bedroom to the right and a small galley kitchen on the left.

"Let's start in the bedroom," suggested Carolina.

Susan followed her. The white French doors to the closet were already open. Susan couldn't help thinking it was almost an invitation to snoop. Dark jeans and a flannel shirt were draped lazily over the closet door.

"I'll start here. You look around the bed and nightstand." The closet smelled like old library books. Susan slid the hangers across the wooden bar one by one. Black pants, dress shirts, jeans and more jeans, a jacket…nothing unusual here. A pair of boots and some black dress shoes were tossed in the bottom of the closet. On the top shelf, Susan saw a few folded sweatshirts and a pair of running shoes.

Meanwhile, Carolina reached under the bed. There was no bedspread—only a blue thermal blanket. Susan watched as Carolina pulled out an empty Vodka bottle. *Poor baby*, thought Susan. She watched as Carolina shook her head and wiped away a tear.

"Check the nightstand," whispered Susan. "Grab anything that might be helpful." Carolina stuffed some crumpled receipts into her coat pocket. Susan eyed the wicker hamper. *Going through Javier's dirty underwear was just a bit too intimate,* she thought. "Carolina, check out the hamper. I'll be in the living room."

Susan lifted the floral couch cushions. She was so focused on finding information to solve Vicky's murder that she jumped when Carolina's voice broke the silence saying, "I think we should check the laptop." Carolina hit the power button. The screen came to life, glowing blue against the dark backdrop of the walls. It was just warming up when all of a sudden they heard the jiggling of keys outside the door.

"What's he doing back so soon? What do we do now?" whispered Carolina. At that moment, Susan noticed a bowling bag next to the coffee table.

Susan's heart was pounding so loudly she was sure Carolina could hear it. She quickly surveyed the apartment. "What's behind those curtains?" asked Susan.

"Sliding glass doors and a balcony." A clank of metal which had to be keys dropping on the floor made them both gasp but bought them a few extra minutes.

"I think that's our best option," said Susan. They raced for the balcony. Carolina unlocked the sliding glass doors. Thank goodness there wasn't a stick in the tract like at home. They scooted out to the balcony sliding the door behind them just as they heard the apartment door opening.

Javier looked a bit disoriented as he paused in the middle of the living room. Carolina and Susan watched through an opening in the curtain as they crouched behind the lawn chairs. Susan realized she'd been holding her breathe as if the sound of breathing would tip Javier off to their presence. Javier made his way into the kitchen and flicked on the light. He yanked open the fridge and took out a Corona.

"Oh, my God," said Carolina. "The computer—we left it on. He never leaves it on when he's not using it."

Susan was now speechless as well as breathless.

"What if he sees it?" asked Carolina.

Javier wandered back into the living room as he took a swig of his beer. He was within arm's length of the laptop as he plopped like a rag doll onto the couch.

"He's going to notice it as soon as he goes for the remote," said Carolina. She was shaking. Susan thought that "shaking with fear" was just an expression but apparently that's exactly what Carolina was doing. Javier took another swig of his beer. Susan's mind was in hyper mode as she evaluated possible escape plans.

When the sound of the phone ringing broke the silence, both Susan and Carolina jumped. Susan bumped her nose on the chair. Javier got up and went into the bedroom to answer the phone. The bedroom door was open but Javier's back was to the living room.

When it became apparent that Javier was engaged in a conversation, Carolina said, "I'll go out first. I'll turn off the computer on the way. If he sees me I'll say I just stopped by to check on him." She pulled open the sliding glass door and glanced over to Javier. Then she crept up to the computer, turned it off and silently unlocked the front door. Then she motioned to Susan.

Susan gently closed the sliding door and ran for the front door. "Phew, I've done my cardio for the day," said Susan when they were safely outside the apartment. They got into the car and headed back to Carolina's. "So did you find anything that could be helpful" asked Susan.

"An empty vodka bottle under the bed—but that's not that unusual these days. I grabbed some receipts and a business card that were in the nightstand drawer." Just then they pulled into the driveway.

"Let me see," said Susan. Carolina pulled the crumpled receipts out of her coat pocket and handed them to Susan. Susan went through them. "Uh oh," said Susan, after a few minutes had passed.

"What is it?"

"This receipt is from the gas station right next to the school. The time and date are from the evening of the concert. Can you think of any reason your dad would be getting gas all the way out there by the school?"

"Only one," said Carolina. "If my dad did kill my mom, I want to see him in jail forever."

Chapter 10

The snow was beginning to fall in bigger flakes as Susan drove Carolina back to her house. Carolina paused as she was about to open the car door. "Please come in for lunch. The housekeeper isn't here on weekends and I don't want to be alone. There are still some casseroles in the fridge."

"I'd love to," said Susan. She turned off the engine and walked up the circular drive with Carolina. Susan had always loved this neighborhood. Each house had about an acre of land and the houses themselves were exquisite. This was not one of those cookie cutter housing developments, no siree. Each house was unique. Carolina lived in a two story Tudor-style with a stone façade. Across the street was a spacious red brick ranch. The windows were trimmed in white. Carolina grabbed the mail on the way in.

"Anything good?" asked Susan.

"Just bills and cards, like usual. Oh, this card is from my Mom's friend Kara. They went to college together at Cornell and have been, I mean had been, friends ever since." Carolina opened the card and read it aloud.

Dear Carolina,

I was devastated to hear the news about your mom. I was out of the country and am so sad that I missed the funeral. Your mom was like a sister to me. She helped me so much—especially when I was having all that trouble with my son John. Please let me know if there is anything I can do for you or your dad.

Love,
Kara

"She is such a sweet lady. Mom loved her." Susan followed Carolina as she went into the kitchen and put a tuna casserole in the microwave. Susan set the table.

"Kara knew how special my mom was. She's probably missing her almost as much as I am." Suddenly they heard a crash.

"What was that?" asked Susan

"I sure don't know. This is usually a super quiet neighborhood. Maybe the wind blew over one of the trash cans."

"That's probably it," said Susan. Only she didn't remember even a hint of wind when they came inside. She remembered the car that she thought was following them earlier and felt the hair on the back of her neck stand up. *If Javier isn't the killer*, she thought, *the real killer is still out there.* Who knows what the true motive for killing Vicky was. Maybe the killer was after something here at the house. Maybe Carolina is in danger. Lynette and Mike always say I have an overactive imagination. I'm sure they're right. She sat down at the blond wooden table with Carolina for lunch.

Chapter 11

Jody Decker was finishing the last of her Christmas shopping with her friend Theresa. The mall was crowded—what did she expect, the weekend before Christmas? Luckily, she had patience—lots of patience. She'd only lived in Westbrook a few months now. When she heard there was an opening at the school, she'd sent in her application the same day. Now here she was with a great job, a new best friend, and her first apartment

"I still need something for my niece," said Theresa. "I'm not sure what size she is so I don't want to buy her clothes."

"Bath and Soaps Shop," said Jody, pointing at the store entrance. "All girls love lotion and shower gel."

Jody and Theresa wandered in. Jody loved the aroma of apples and cinnamon that embraced them as soon as they crossed the threshold. She suddenly craved apple pie. Before long, both women had a cacophony of scents climbing up their arms.

"I need to get my mother a little something else too." Jody picked up a lotion she hadn't seen before. "Melatonin Melon. It's supposed to help with jet lag. Mom could really use that. She just came back from a trip to Africa last week and said it took her three days to get over the jet lag." Jody put it in her straw basket along with the matching shower gel and a net sponge. In spite of the fact that every register was open, the line was ten customers deep. Ahead of them, a woman must have had thirty bottles of shower gels and body mists.

After standing in line for what seemed like an eternity, Jody and Theresa headed to the food court for a treat. Jody chose a walnut brownie.

"I'm going to be a rebel and get the one with nuts," said Jody.

Theresa laughed. "Why not, we're on vacation now." Nuts were forbidden at school because of children with allergies.

"Who had ever heard of a magnet school specifically for kids with nut allergies?" said Jody.

"Well, there are plenty of nuts at school—just not the edible kind," joked Theresa. She ordered a pecan chocolate chip cookie. The food court was teeming with shoppers but they eventually found a table.

"I heard that Vicky was covered in bruises when they found her," said Theresa. "Poor lady. Do you think Antonio Petrocelli had anything to do with it? I heard a rumor that he and Vicky were having an affair. Remember that core curriculum summit they went to? I heard they never left her hotel room."

"Maybe it was Antonio's wife then." Jody raised her eyebrows and emphasized the word wife. "Actually, I think it was that wacko parent Blaze Conrad." She fanned her perfectly manicured nails out in front of her.

"You know, maybe it wasn't even murder. She could have just dropped dead from a blood clot or something," said Theresa.

"I don't know. My money is on murder though. From what I hear, she deserved to die for some of the evil things she did to people." Jody felt her face turn red.

"Wow, Jody, that's not like you. You usually see the good in everyone."

"Yeah, you're right." Jody sighed. "The stress has gotten to me. Let's head out. I still have some wrapping to do."

Chapter 12

"Come on, Lynette. I'll drive," said Jackson. He put on his jacket and tied his knitted scarf around his neck.

Jackson and Lynette got into the cruiser and rode downtown to the movie theater. The theater was old and smelled like damp towels mixed with stale popcorn. Paint was peeling off the walls in spots. They walked in and passed the glass concession stand with the overpriced Snow Caps and Raisinettes. When they approached the only person they saw who appeared to be past the legal drinking age, Jackson pulled out the photo he'd taken of Blaze Conrad.

"Excuse me, sir. We're from the Westbrook Police Department." Jackson flashed his badge. "We're investigating a murder. We were wondering if you recognize this man." He handed the photo to the young man who he assumed was the manager.

"I don't recognize him but lots of people come through these doors. He may have been here. I can't say for sure."

"I understand," said Jackson.

Lynette and Jackson then showed the picture to the girls working at the concession stand. One wore a Westbrook High sweatshirt. The other was dressed in a plaid flannel shirt. Lynette whispered in Jackson's ear, "What ever happened to dressing appropriately for work? Didn't their parents teach them anything about making a good impression?"

"We worked that night but I don't remember him. I've usually got a good memory for faces," said the one with the freckles. "At least that's what my mom says."

Next, they tried the teenager at the ticket window. "Do you remember seeing this man Monday night?" said Jackson. "He would have bought a ticket for the James Bond film. He was alone." The popping of hot corn kernels and the buttery aroma emanating from the concession stand made Jackson's stomach growl.

"No." He paused. "Wait a minute. Did you say the James Bond film?"

"Yes," replied Jackson.

"Well, that would have been impossible. The projector in that theater broke Sunday afternoon, right in the middle of the movie. We didn't get it fixed till yesterday."

"Thank you," said Jackson. "You've been very helpful." He smiled at Lynette.

Jackson and Lynette headed back to the car. "I say we pick him up," said Jackson. "If he isn't guilty, then why would he lie about where he was that night?"

"I know. He might as well have said he was alone watching TV. He had to know no one would have seen him at the movies," said Lynette.

Jackson checked for Blaze's address. The snow was falling a little harder now and the sky was smoky gray. They stopped back at the station to finish some paperwork. Lynette put on a fresh pot of coffee. A few hours later they knocked on Blaze's door.

"I'm coming already." Blaze looked through chain locked door and then opened it for them. "What are you doing here?" said Blaze. He was wearing jeans and a flannel shirt. There were toy cars on the floor near the television and a leapfrog learning pad on the coffee table, but judging from the quietness in the house, Ryan must have been either with his mom or at school.

"Good afternoon, Mr. Conrad. How are you doing today?" asked Jackson.

"Just dandy, thank you," answered Blaze. The suspicion in his tone was obvious.

"I'm afraid you'll need to come downtown with us for another round of questioning. You've become a person of interest in the Victoria Rogers murder case," said Jackson. He pulled up his pants that kept slipping down beneath his belly.

"What kind of bull is that? I didn't do nothing. What gives you the right to harass me?" said Blaze.

"We checked phone records. You called Mrs. Rogers' cell phone half a dozen times in the week preceding the murder. Sandra, the school secretary, says you were in her office the day of the murder threatening to get even with her," said Jackson.

"Yes, because I found new evidence proving that she knew about the molester. I was heading back to my lawyer with it. The school social worker told me that there had been a similar incident with another child. I was giving her one last chance to admit it before hiring a private investigator. That social worker, Miss Decker, wouldn't give me a name."

"We also checked your background and saw that you have a record for assault and battery." Jackson puffed out his chest, proud that he'd uncovered that bit of info.

"That was fifteen years ago. It was just a frickin' bar fight" He sounded as if his blood were boiling. "You people are just looking for a scapegoat. I know how it works. You want to show the public you solved this case so you grab the first easy target you can get your hands on."

"Mr. Conrad," said Jackson, "I strongly suggest you cooperate and perhaps speak to your lawyer."

Chapter 13

How is it possible that two people generate so much laundry? Susan tossed the sheets and pillowcases into the hamper and brought in new ones from the linen closet. She loved the 'country fresh fragrance' of the new brand of detergent she'd bought. The sheets made her think of a day in a country garden—just like the commercial said. "Get down, Johann." The cats didn't mind jumping on the sheets while Susan was in the process of making the bed. They figured she'd work around them, and she usually did just that. Carolina called while she was smoothing out the blue and white bedspread that matched the color of the walls. Susan had read that painting your bedroom blue helped people sleep better. She could barely understand what Carolina was saying. Carolina was crying and talking simultaneously.

"Can you come over and help me go through some of my Mom's things? I want to see if we can find anyone else who may have had a motive to kill her. I know it can't be my dad. What if he goes to jail?"

Susan couldn't say no to Carolina. She didn't want her to have to cope with her Dad going to jail. What was that expression? Something about adding insult to an injury?

She was determined to find Vicky's killer and give her some sort of closure.

"Calm down, honey. I'll be over in about an hour," she told Carolina. Mike came out of the shower just as she was hanging up.

"Oh, what a hunk," said Susan.

"Aren't you lucky to have me?" joked Mike. He quickly opened then closed his terry towel.

After thirty six years of marriage, Susan still thought he was a hottie. 'They'd had their ups and downs but she couldn't imagine life without him. That's why she had a hard time believing you could get so angry with your spouse that you could murder him or her. Could Javier have really murdered Vicky? She squeezed Mike's butt as he walked to the dresser. He reciprocated with a kiss.

"I'm going over to Carolina's to look for clues." She'd already shared her experience at Javier's apartment.

"I think you should tell Lynette and let her handle this. You're going to wind up in danger. If there's a killer out there, he won't appreciate you snooping around."

"I'll be fine. Besides, it's not like I have a bunch of things on my 'to do' list. I want to help Carolina."

"What time will you be back? Want to go out for dinner tonight? I'm craving Chinese."

"Sounds like a plan. I'll be back in plenty of time for dinner. I've even got a coupon for China Garden."

Susan drove the short distance to Carolina's house. At least the housekeeper was there today. She really didn't understand why Javier hadn't moved back into the house. Maybe he wanted the freedom to get drunk and lounge around without being subjected to the scrutiny of his daughter. She couldn't imagine not being there for your child. She hadn't been a perfect mother to Lynette and Evan but she sure tried to do her best. It wasn't always easy working full time and raising her own kids but she did it. Susan parked in the circular driveway, locked the car, and rang the doorbell. Carolina let her in. She gave her a hug.

"I'm going to find out who really killed my mom," said Carolina. She'd obviously been crying but now her voice had a definite tone of determination. "I pulled out a box of photos and some folders full of papers from my mom's bedroom. We can start there," said Carolina.

Carolina spread the photos out on the coffee table. There were a lot to go through. "This is me at the debate tournament. I remember that day. I was trying extemp although I usually do oratory. I did terribly because I hadn't brought in my own research. That's the last debate tournament my mom will ever hear. I wish I'd done a better job."

"Well, at least you're human. It's okay not to always be perfect," said Susan.

"My mom was not happy. I know she was embarrassed. I can't stand that she isn't here with me anymore. I want her to see my tournaments, and my graduation. I want her to be there when I decide where I'm going to college." Carolina began to sob.

"I know how hard this is. I wish I could take away the hurt. I'll do everything I can to help solve your Mom's murder." She picked up a photo. "Where was this taken?" asked Susan.

"That's Mom and Dad at a friend's wedding. That's the Roosevelt Mansion. The grounds are beautiful. We used to picnic there sometimes." She picked up another handful of photos. "These are from last Christmas. After we opened presents, Mom and Dad had a huge fight. Dad stormed out. When he came back later he'd clearly been drinking." After going through boxes of photos, Carolina pulled out some albums.

"These are from when she was younger," said Carolina. They looked through her wedding album, albums from when Carolina was a baby, and albums of trips they'd taken as a family. Carolina looked so sad. Susan could tell that she was swallowing her tears.

Then Carolina pulled out a leather-covered album from maybe twenty years ago. It was from before she was born.

"Look," said Carolina. This is a picture of mom's friend Kara, the one I got the letter from. "This must be at Kara's house." She showed Susan a picture of a woman maybe in her thirties with a teenage boy. *The boy was gawky-looking and going through that pimply teenage cocoon stage,* thought Susan. Kids go from being adorable to looking and acting like aliens from another planet. Then, sometime around when they go to college, they undergo a metamorphosis…sometimes. Carolina was lucky. She didn't have a spot of acne on her olive skin and she was already beautiful inside and out. She reminded Susan of Lynette at that age, except Lynette was blonde and fair skinned. And Carolina was so quiet. Lynette had been rather mouthy.

"By the time I was old enough to know her, Mom had moved away from Ithaca to Westbrook and Kara was traveling a lot for her job. She was involved in some kind of missionary work. I only met her a few times." The picture was taken in a country-style kitchen. Kara and her son were standing in front of a butcher block table. Kara was wearing a red and white gingham apron with an appliqué of a dog bone on the bodice. The auburn-haired boy was wearing tight jeans and a Jets jersey. His shaggy hair fell into his face. She could see by his expression that he'd wanted to be anywhere else but there.

"Let's have some lunch," suggested Carolina. "There's lasagna that's been in the freezer since the funeral. I haven't had much of an appetite." She popped two servings into the microwave.

"Thanks," said Susan. "I'll pour us some iced tea."

"I have to know who did this to my Mom. It won't bring her back, but at least I'll know my Mom's killer will suffer the consequences."

"Carolina, you know how much I care about you. I will do everything in my power to get to the bottom of this. Let's get back to work."

"Let's explore her bedroom," suggested Carolina. Carolina led Susan up the stairs and into the expansive master bedroom. The floor was hard wood and covered with a red and gold oriental area rug. The bed was queen-sized; an antique four poster covered with a down comforter and enough pillows to supply a preschool class at naptime. Oddly enough, the bedposts had carved pineapples on the top. Susan did remember reading somewhere that pineapples were supposed to be a sign of hospitality. There was an antique rolled-top desk in the corner near the bed. Susan tried to open it but the top was locked.

"Do you have a key?" asked Susan.

"No. I didn't even know she kept it locked." Carolina searched the dresser drawers and jewelry box looking for a key. Meanwhile, Susan tried to pry it open with her hands. Carolina searched through shoe boxes on top of the closet but all she found were shoes.

"No luck," she said.

"Me neither." said Susan, "But I think maybe if we had a screw driver or something to pry it open with we may be able to open it."

"My dad has a toolbox on the back porch. I'll go look for one."

"You know, your hands are more nimble than mine. You work on the lock and I'll go get it." Susan ran down the steps (this counted as cardio, right?), opened the sliding glass door, and stepped out onto the porch. It was freezing outside without a jacket. Then she stopped and bent down. *I wonder where these footprints came from. They look recent. Maybe Araceli had come out here for some reason.* Susan shivered and decided to get back to the task at hand. She rummaged through the toolbox but couldn't find a single screwdriver. Then she went back into the kitchen, foraged through the silverware drawer, and grabbed a butter knife.

"This should do," said Susan when she came back to the bedroom.

"I'll give it a try," said Carolina.

After working on it for a few minutes, the lock broke open. Cubbies were assigned to pens, pencils, stamps, and notepads. There was even a quaint letter opener placed neatly across the desktop. Susan couldn't help comparing it to her own desk, which had piles of papers, old mail, and a can for scissors and glue sticks that were mostly dried out and useless.

"Your mom was very organized."

"A place for everything and everything in its place. That was mom's motto." Then Carolina noticed a cell phone. "Mom had a different cell phone. It had a Burberry case. I don't know whose this is."

"Let's turn it on." Susan was surprised that it still held a charge. A picture of Vicky and Carolina appeared on the screen.

"What's that?" asked Carolina.

"Well, this is strange. Let's look through and see if we find anything useful. It may contain a clue," said Susan. They began to go through the calls and messages. It became obvious that it did belong to Vicky.

"There are very few people in her contacts. Who did she list as *boy toy*?" said Carolina.

Susan snatched the phone from Carolina's hand. She scrolled down and saw an entry for the Omni Hotel. *The nearest Omni must be in Manhattan* she thought. There certainly wasn't one here in Westbrook. She also saw an entry for The Hilton. Then there was another cryptic listing—*macho man. Looks like maybe there was another side to Vicky that no one knew about*, thought Susan. She handed it back to Carolina.

"Can you find the messages?"

"Yes, here are her texts. This one is from October. It says, "*Meet me at the bar in 10.*" The reply says "*Already waiting.*" Later there's one saying how much fun it was to be away from school and how much more fun she could expect. She answers, "*You better be super careful that this stays between us.*" Here's another one from *macho man: "You won't get away with this. I'll find you.*" And this one says, *I'll always be your baby boy—can't wait till our next play date.*

"That one from *Macho Man* sounds a bit ominous. I guess now I know my dad is a drunk and my mom was a slut. I don't believe it. How much more can I take?" She started crying. Susan comforted her although she kind of agreed with the slut part. She herself couldn't imagine cheating on Mike. Her heart ached for Carolina.

"She must have had her reasons, Carolina. She was still a great mom to you even if she wasn't the best wife." Susan put the phone down and looked through the papers that were neatly stacked on the desk.

"This is a restraining order against your dad."

"I told you he was getting violent. She must have been worried that he'd hurt us, even though she kept reassuring me that he wasn't a threat."

Susan continued through the pile. "These look like divorce papers," said Susan.

"I didn't think it had gotten that far," said Carolina. She looked down at the floor. Susan thought she saw a tear. "I guess we hit the jackpot."

"Well, the impending divorce may have given your dad a stronger motive. I know he was jobless and counted on your mom's paycheck. However, there was obviously a third party involved. It sounds like *boy toy* was rather angry. A fourth if you include *macho man.* And who is *baby boy*? Maybe they too had motives. I'm going to have to go to Lynette with this. I'm sorry, Carolina."

"No, I knew that was probably going to happen. It was only a matter of time."

Susan hated leaving Carolina. She looked so sad and so vulnerable. Maybe it wasn't Javier after all. Maybe it was this newly discovered boyfriend. Or *macho man.* Or maybe it was Blaze Conrad. It was time to get Lynette up to speed with what they'd discovered—first thing in the morning. Right now she had a dinner date.

Chapter 14

Susan woke up early as usual. She hopped on the treadmill while she watched the morning news. *I'll use a little incline since I had that sweet and sour chicken last night,* she thought. She hit a button and the treadmill rose slightly. She jacked up the volume on the TV so she could hear it above the sound of the motor.

"Bye, I'll see you at dinnertime," said Mike. "I'd kiss you goodbye but I just took a shower."

"Okay; you owe me then," said Susan. She wasn't looking forward to sharing what she'd learned about Javier with the police. The morning show was featuring a chef demonstrating how to make a cake using black beans and Diet Coke. *How disgusting,* she thought. *I'd rather eat mud.* She took her shower, ate breakfast (oatmeal again), and then headed to the station where she was greeted by Jackson.

"Hello, Jackson. Can I please speak with Lynette?"

With his doughy face, Jackson reminded Susan of a gargoyle. "She's not here right now. She had a doctor's appointment. She should be back anytime. Can I help you?" He emphasized the word *I.*

Susan didn't want to talk to Jackson. He was so condescending whenever she mentioned anything about a case. *Lynette was so much better at being a detective than Jackson could ever hope to be,* thought Susan.

"I'll wait." Susan took a seat on one of the hard plastic chairs in the waiting area.

"Have some insights for us? Playing Jessica Fletcher again? You should be playing bridge and knitting."

Just then, Lynette came in. She didn't look happy. She and Jason had been trying to have a baby for a while now. Susan could see by her expression that things hadn't gone well at the doctor. Susan couldn't wait to have a grandchild, especially now that she had the time to enjoy one, but all in good time. Maybe they'd wind up adopting. Her dental hygienist's daughter had recently adopted a little girl from China. She had shown her a picture. Susan was fine with the idea of a delicate little granddaughter with a mop of black hair. They could go to the park and go shopping. She smiled inside.

"Hi, Mom; what can I do for you?"

"Can we talk in private?" She darted her eyes in Jackson's direction and back, hoping Lynette would get the hint.

"Sure, come into my office."

Susan followed Lynette. Lynette's office was cozy in spite of the utilitarian desk and chair. A wedding picture and a colorful, hand-painted paperweight that said *Acapulco* helped personalize the space. Susan wanted to start by saying how sorry she was that things hadn't gone well at the doctor but she knew from experience that Lynette would just get more upset.

"Carolina and I went through some of Vicky's things. We found out that she'd taken out a restraining order against Javier and that she'd filed for divorce."

"We knew about the restraining order. The husband is always on the suspect list when the wife has been murdered. We also interviewed a neighbor who says she heard screaming coming from the house on more than one occasion. She says they fought a lot. No one saw Javier at the crime scene though. We have no reason to believe he was anywhere near the school that night."

"Well, actually…" Susan wrung her hands in her lap. "Carolina and I found a receipt showing that he was at the gas station around the corner that night."

"You *found* a receipt? How did you happen to find it and why didn't you tell me this before?"

"I promised Carolina we'd look for more information first."

"Go on," said Lynette.

"Well." Susan squirmed in her seat. "When we went through Vicky's things, like I said, we found the restraining order and divorce papers."

"Divorce papers?" said Lynette.

"Yes. I think you should dig a little deeper. At best, you can prove he's innocent."

"Thanks for telling me how to do my job, Mom. I'll get on it. No more snooping though. How's that scrap booking project coming along? "

Susan knew this was a good time to make her exit. She walked out of Lynette's office. Jackson was sitting at the front desk.

"Thanks for stopping by Mrs. Wiles. What would we do without you?"

Susan wanted to wipe that sarcastic grin right off Jackson's face but all she needed was to be locked up for assaulting a police officer. Instead, she said, "Bye Jackson, have a Merry Christmas."

Chapter 15

On the way home, Susan decided to stop at Safeway to buy groceries for Christmas dinner. *Let's see, I'll need a turkey, a small honey-glazed ham, potatoes, stuffing, and green beans,* thought Susan. Maybe she would also buy some refrigerated cinnamon rolls and bacon to have for Christmas breakfast. The store wasn't very crowded judging by the abundance of parking spaces. There was a display of fresh Christmas trees at the store entrance. Susan took a deliberate breath and drank in the aroma of fresh evergreens. She grabbed a grocery cart, wiped it down with the sanitary wipes the store now provided, and headed for the cinnamon rolls. Of course, she first had to stop and admire the poinsettias at the store entrance, rifle through the bin of colorful wrapping paper rolls, and check out the display of frosted Christmas cookies. She couldn't help thinking that even grocery shopping was more fun during holiday time. Maybe she'd buy a tray of those cookies to send to Evan. He always did prefer store bought cookies to homemade. She wished that he could get away from med school for Christmas this year but it wasn't possible.

Susan grabbed the cinnamon rolls and bacon. As she headed to the meat department, she saw a familiar face. At first she couldn't place him, but then she realized that it was Blaze Conrad. He'd helped her set up the stage when Ryan was in the kindergarten program. *Why is he grocery shopping in the middle of the day? Shouldn't he be at work? Maybe he'd lost his job.*

Maybe he'd lost his job because he got angry and punched a coworker. See, there was that violent streak again. He probably did kill Vicky. And who's that blond woman he's with? I remember his wife and that isn't her. I'll bet Javier is innocent after all. That would be a huge relief for Carolina.

Susan decided to follow Blaze and the blond woman into the bakery section where an elderly woman in a Santa hat was handing out samples of fruit cake. *Oh, my gosh,* thought Susan. Did she just really see what she thought she saw? The blond lady had taken a sample of fruitcake and fed it to Blaze. Yep, she put it right into his mouth. If Blaze was capable of cheating on his wife then maybe he was capable of murder too. Susan remembered how he'd been quoted in the newspaper as saying what a stable and happy home life Ryan had. He had insisted that Ryan's behavioral problems were due to being molested at the school. This was during the time when the lawsuit against Vicky and the school district was happening. She decided to keep following them.

Blaze and his girlfriend turned down the cereal aisle. Now they appeared to be arguing. Susan didn't want to get too close. She couldn't hear what they were saying but could tell by their body language that something was going on. Susan tossed a box of Kashi cereal into her cart. Then she followed them down the bread aisle. Blaze put a loaf of Wonder Bread into his cart.

"Don't you dare tell me what I should or shouldn't do," Blaze shouted to the blond.

"I'm not, but you know better," she responded.

"Shut up right now or you'll be sorry," said Blaze.

"But you..." said the blond. Before she could finish, Blaze hauled off and smacked her right across the face. The blond woman's hand went immediately to her cheek. Susan could see that she was in pain but the woman held back her tears. She left Blaze with the cart and started toward the store exit. Blaze caught up with her.

"I'm sorry. Are you okay? I didn't mean to do that. Come on, baby, I said I'm sorry." Blaze pleaded with his girlfriend. After a few minutes, they were hugging and going back into the store.

At the checkout, Susan chose a line adjacent to the one Blaze and the mystery blond were in. It was as if the smacking incident had never happened. She nonchalantly watched as Blaze loaded a bottle of wine, strawberries, and a hunk of imported cheese onto the conveyor belt. *Hmm, I don't see any Oreos or Frosted Flakes*, thought Susan. Obviously Blaze wasn't shopping for his son. As she was watching, Blaze suddenly turned and glared at her. She quickly turned her head and pretended to be choosing from the rack of disposable razor blades next to her. She doubted that Blaze had gotten a good look at her. Even if he had, it had been over a year since he'd last seen her and she was wearing a hat. Did she dare follow him in her car? Maybe she'd discover something that would tie him into Vicky's murder if she did. She owed it to Carolina. She had to prove that Javier was innocent for Carolina's sake.

She quickly loaded her groceries into the Prius and slumped behind the wheel. When Blaze pulled out of the parking lot, she followed, keeping a safe distance between them. She got caught at a red light but was still able to catch up to him. Eventually, he pulled into an apartment complex. Susan followed him and pulled into a visitor's parking space. Blaze and the blond grabbed their bag of groceries and started down the sidewalk. They were obviously together. Susan craned her neck out her car window to see which apartment they were going to. Then the unexpected happened. Blaze handed the grocery bag to the blond, did a 180, and ran down the sidewalk toward Susan's car. Susan's heart pounded. She briefly fumbled with the car key, then started the engine and high tailed it out of the parking lot. She could see Blaze running after her. He appeared to be yelling. *There was that violent streak again,* thought Susan. When he was clearly out of sight, Susan began to breathe normally and headed home. She had a moment of panic when she realized that Blaze had gotten a good look at her car. She'd have to be more careful. Blaze was looking pretty suspicious and she had no idea what he might be capable of.

Chapter 16

The sun glistened on the shimmery snow outside the Petrocelli house. The sky was clear and blue. It was a perfect day to celebrate Christmas. Tony came running into his parents' bedroom. At least he'd waited for the sun to come up this year.

"Mommy, Daddy, Santa came!" Tony bounced on the king-sized bed trying to get Antonio and Hayley to wake up.

"Okay partner, we're coming," said Antonio. Hayley tied her satin bathrobe and put on her gold toned slippers.

"I think I'll make us some pancakes and bacon. Maybe I'll go buy some oranges and squeeze them into juice. Then we can open presents."

"No, Mommy, no! I want to open them now."

"I was just kidding, honey. You know I wouldn't make you wait."

"I kind of like the fresh-squeezed orange juice idea though," said Antonio. Hayley gave him a playful swat on the head. "I hear the baby. Go on down and I'll get him. Then we can open presents."

Hayley went into the baby's room. She scooped him up and put him on the changing table. "Your first Christmas, kiddo." After she changed his diaper, she snapped him into a onesie that said 'Baby's First Christmas.' She thought about the day Cory was born. Antonio was at school when her water broke. She called his cell but he didn't answer. Then she called the school. He was supposed to be helping Vicky that day but no one could find him. She actually had to ask her neighbor to drive her to the hospital. Antonio didn't show up until hours later. She'd had a good idea where he was. She was sure he and Vicky had slipped out for a long lunch followed by a nap in the motel by the mall. Antonio had no idea that she was on to him. He was going to pay for cheating on her and he wouldn't even see it coming.

***

Jody Decker woke up early to a clean blanket of snow outside the window. Later in the spring it would look all dirty and slushy. Dirty snow always put her in a foul mood. She put on the new gray sweater dress she'd bought while Christmas shopping with Theresa. Theresa always teased her about being such a girlie girl. *Love the way this hugs my curves,* she thought—even if I am only going to visit my mom. *And I love this new gel polish.* She fanned her nails out in front of her. *I can't believe this French manicure has lasted almost two weeks now.* Next she fussed with her hair. *Hmmm,* thought Jody. *Up in a loose bun or flowing down my back?* Jody decided to put it up. It would stay neater during the long drive. She put on some fashionable boots. She preferred heels but the snow made it a little hard to walk outside in them. She decided to throw a pair into her overnight bag just in case. She called her Mom to tell her she was about to leave.

"Hi, Mom. Yes, I had a nice time with Theresa and her family last night. Midnight Mass was beautiful. Theresa's family took up an entire pew. I'm about to leave. I know, I haven't been home since moving here but I'll see you in a few hours." Jody and her mom had gone through some stormy times in the past. Jody was glad that they were able to maintain a relationship now that she was an adult. Jody ended the call and closed her suitcase.

Then she gave Theresa a quick call to say goodbye and wish her a Merry Christmas. Theresa was a good friend. It was nice that she included her in her family's plans. Jody didn't make friends that easily. Ever since childhood, she'd had trouble fitting in with others. For a while she really tried to be like the other kids. She even pretended to care about watching football games and buying the latest CDs. Then she gave up. Theresa understood her though. There was a real connection there. Jody got into her car and started on her trip.

***

Susan had the turkey in the oven and was mashing potatoes. There was nothing like the aroma of turkey roasting in the oven. She loved the holidays. She couldn't help feeling sad that Evan wouldn't be home this year but there would be plenty of future holidays. Some day he'd be a world class surgeon publishing in *The New England Journal of Medicine* and flying to Paris to speak at medical conventions. And she'd be getting some really cool Christmas gift from him—maybe a cabin in Rhode Island. Then they could all have family reunions up there in the summer. He'd be there with his future family enjoying a well deserved rest from his hectic schedule and Lynette and Jason would be there with her little Chinese granddaughter. The doorbell rang and she heard Mike greeting Lynette and Jason. They'd stopped to pick up Carolina. Susan didn't expect that Javier would be cooking Christmas dinner. In fact, she'd invited him to come over too but he had declined.

Susan gave Lynette, Jason, and Carolina hugs and kisses. "Merry Christmas,"

She said. "I'm so glad you're all here." Susan noticed that Carolina looked even sadder than usual. She wasn't surprised given that this was her first

Christmas without her mom. She led them into the living room.

"Have a seat. Help yourselves to drinks. There's soda or wine," said Susan.

Mike brought in a tray of hot canapés. "These are delicious; you have to try some," he said. He put the tray down on the coffee table.

"Lynette, I could use some help," said Susan.

"Of course, Mom." Lynette followed her into the kitchen.

"Lynette, I think you really need to look at Blaze Conrad very closely as a suspect. I happened to see him at Safeway the other day. He was with a young blond woman who I know isn't his wife. You know how he painted such a Norman Rockwell picture of his family during the trial."

"Mom, you have no idea who that woman was. She could have been his sister for all you know."

"No, she most definitely wasn't his sister. They were all lovey-dovey with each other before the incident."

"Incident? What the heck are you talking about?" said Lynette.

"Well, they started arguing with each other right smack in the middle of the bread aisle. Blaze hit her right across the face—hard."

"What does that prove other than that Blaze is a first class jerk?"

"It proves he has a violent streak. He could have easily gotten mad at Vicky and killed her the night of the concert."

"Mom, we have no reason to believe Blaze was at the school that night. You're grasping at straws. Leave the investigation to the police. I wish you'd trust me to do my job."

"Of course, I trust you. You're the best detective on that police force. I just want to help, that's all. I know how busy things get for you."

"I appreciate it but you have to stop meddling." Lynette opened the oven and stuck the meat thermometer into the turkey's thigh. "It looks like this bird is ready to eat. I can't wait. Let's get dad in here to carve it."

"Okay, but help me get these potatoes and green beans out on the table in the meantime," said Susan.

***

While Carolina was trying to get through the day with Susan's family, Javier was frantically throwing clothes into his suitcase. He searched through the drawer for that business card but couldn't find it. Then he remembered he'd entered the number in his phone.

"Yes, I'll be there today. No, no contact information. This has to be discreet."

Javier grabbed the laptop and his suitcases. *This house of cards was about to be blown down. Carolina didn't deserve this.* He turned off the lights, locked the door, and loaded his jeep. It was going to be a long drive. He tried to find a gas station that was open on Christmas Day. Eventually, he pulled into a Shell station. The mini-mart was open which was good because by this time Javier was starving. He grabbed a bag of chips, a Snickers bar and a Sprite. *Great Christmas dinner* he thought. It was all Vicky's fault. When he found out that she was cheating on him he blew up. She literally drove him to drink. The last straw was when he'd gotten the summons about the divorce. Divorce? They'd never even discussed that. Besides, he was the one who should have been initiating a divorce. He may be an alcoholic but at least he'd never cheated on her. A divorce would have been devastating. It was already humiliating that she'd made him move out and had prepaid a rental for him. If they were divorced he didn't know what he'd live on. When he received those papers he was more than furious. He'd called Vicky's cell but she didn't answer.

Then he remembered there was a concert at the school that night. He jumped into the jeep and high tailed it over there. Of course, he hadn't realized that the gas light was on so he had to make a stop first. Didn't stop his momentum though. When he arrived at the school, the parking lot was full. He could hear the concert as soon as he walked in the door. *Feliz Navidad*...fat chance. Feeling like a volcano about to erupt, he went to her office and waited for her. She was so smug. "You're history, my soon to be ex-hubby. You're a sorry excuse for a man—alcoholic, you lost your job. You even look like you slept under a bridge." That's what she told him. Then he let her have it. Javier got back on the highway and never looked back.

Chapter 16

The next morning, the phone rang while Susan was unloading the dishwasher.

"Mrs. W., I'm so worried," said Carolina. "I didn't know who else to call."

"What's wrong?" Carolina sounded frantic and Susan knew it took a lot to rattle her.

"I tried to call my dad. He didn't answer. I called all morning. Finally, I decided to go over there and make sure he was okay. The housekeeper took me over there. I knocked but he didn't answer so I let myself in. It looked like a ghost town in there. Everything that belonged to my dad was gone. I'm sure he wouldn't just go away without telling me. We'd talked about getting together after Christmas so I know he didn't plan on going away."

"Maybe he had a job interview out of town."

"He wouldn't have packed all his things then."

"Carolina, let me call Lynette. He might be in trouble." Susan was thinking that Javier was either on a drunken binge, or he was trying to hide from the police. Maybe he had murdered Vicky after all. She'd only met him that once. It's possible that he was crazy enough to kill his wife because she was cheating on him or because he was unemployed and facing a divorce.

"Okay. Go ahead and call her. Maybe he had been drinking, decided to leave town, and gotten into an accident. He could be dead just like my mom."

Susan thought it unlikely that Carolina was suddenly an orphan but did think it was about time to involve the police. She hung up with Carolina and called Lynette.

"Lynette, can you come over? It's police business. It's about Vicky's murder."

"What is it now, Mom?" Susan detected a bit of sarcasm in her daughter's voice.

"I can't talk about it over the phone but it's serious."

"It's always serious. Okay, I'll be right there," said Lynette.

Meanwhile, Susan picked up Carolina. She thought Lynette might want to question her. Susan's mind started working. She was seeing a police chase complete with sirens. Lynette would be behind the wheel skillfully dodging cars in her pursuit of Javier. It would be just like the OJ Simpson case except Lynette would be chasing a jeep instead of a white bronco. A knock at the door brought her back to the moment. It was Lynette.

"Thanks for coming so quickly." She put her hands on Carolina's shoulder. "Carolina couldn't get in touch with her dad so she went over to his apartment and when she got there it looked as if he'd moved out."

Lynette addressed her questions to Carolina. "What makes you say that? Did he have plans to move?"

"No, he never said anything about moving. His closet and drawers were empty and the sheets and blanket were off of the bed. All his suitcases, his bowling bowl, and his laptop were gone."

"We know about the impending divorce and that he was near the school the night of the murder. Can you think of anything else that could help us find him?" asked Lynette.

"I don't think so." Carolina reached into her coat pocket. "Wait, I found this on his nightstand. It's probably nothing." It was the business card. She handed it to Lynette.

"This is simply a name and phone number. It's impossible to tell what relevance this has, but I'll take this back to the station and look into it," said Lynette. "We should be getting the complete coroner's report any time now also. The holidays have really delayed things. To top it off, the medical examiner went to Minnesota to visit his family and the airports are still not open. They're calling it the blizzard of the century. I'll keep you in the loop." Lynette headed back to the station.

Chapter 17

"Hey, Jackson, let's see if we can figure out who Dr. Robert Manning is. Vicky's daughter found this business card but there isn't any other info on it. Also, Javier, the husband, seems to have skipped town. He took his things and left his apartment without a word to his daughter." Lynette poured herself a cup of coffee. "Did we get the report back from the medical examiner yet? It sure is taking a while."

"Nope, still waiting," answered Jackson.

"Did you ask Theresa Rizzo out on a date yet?"

"No. I can't imagine her wanting to go out with me. She's so beautiful; I bet she can get anyone she wants." Jackson got on the computer and started googling Dr. Robert Manning. Meanwhile, Lynette tried to trace Javier's cell phone. A well-dressed blonde woman who looked to be in her mid thirties walked into the station. She wore dark wash jeans and a leather jacket.

"I'm looking for one of the detectives working on the Victoria Rogers case," said the blonde woman.

Lynnette and Jackson stopped working and came to the counter. "I'm detective Lynette Sanders and this is my partner Jackson Simpson. We're both working on the Rogers case. How can we help you?"

She unlatched the door in the counter and showed the woman into her office. Jackson followed.

"I have some information relevant to the case. It's about Blaze Conrad. I understand he's a person of interest in this case."

"Yes, go on," said Lynette.

"He's definitely not guilty. He didn't murder that principal."

"And what makes you so certain?" said Jackson.

"Because he was with me that night at my apartment. My next door neighbor can verify that. She was walking her toy poodle. I'm his girlfriend."

"Why didn't he tell us if he had an alibi?" said Jackson.

"Because he and his wife are having custody issues over Ryan. He was so afraid that it would hurt him if his wife knew he was already seeing someone. They aren't even legally divorced yet. I told him I'd keep his secret but when he said he was a suspect in a murder case I figured it was in Ryan's best interest not to have his dad in jail."

"Can you give us your name and address? We'll go check out Mr. Conrad's new alibi. If we can verify that he was indeed with you that night perhaps we can eliminate him as a suspect. Thank you for coming in." Lynette walked her out. She then turned her attention to Jackson.

"Let's go. If this checks out, it looks like Javier Rogers is our number one suspect," said Lynette.

Chapter 18

Jody grabbed her mail and newspapers then turned on the light to her apartment. The apartment looked like a freshly-cleaned hotel room. Everything was immaculate, the sheets changed, the floor vacuumed. Jody would have had a plastic wrapped cup in the bathroom had it been possible. She turned up the heat. *Home sweet home*, she thought. She had gotten through this visit with her mom more smoothly than usual, maybe because they'd spent half of the time at her mom's church. Her mom had dragged her to bible study and even a choir rehearsal while she was visiting. The church had become the center of her mom's life after her father's death years ago. Lately, she'd gotten into missionary work. Jody remembered how every time there was a problem in their household when she was growing up, her mom would actually ask her," What do you think Jesus would do? " Jody rolled her eyes just thinking about it.

Jody unpacked and tossed her dirty clothes directly into the washing machine. Tomorrow it was back to school. *You know that Sunday night feeling when you realize the weekend is over and you have to go to work the next day? Coming back after a vacation was that feeling on steroids. It was like jumping into a cold pool. You dread it, you plunge in, and after a while you just adjust.* Maybe she'd give Theresa a call and see if they could grab a quick dinner. Jody's mom was a talented cook and had sent her home with a goody bag but Jody needed company. Maybe Becky, her new friend from the gym, would join them too.

Chapter 19

Monday morning came too soon.

"Good morning, Mr. Petrocelli," said Sandra. "How was your break?"

"It was wonderful. I got to spend lots of quality time with Hayley and the boys. And yours?"

"My son came down with his family. The grandkids have grown so much in just a few months. Ate too much and spent too much though," said Sandra.

"They don't call it vacation for nothing," said Antonio.

Mr. Ford, the assistant principal, was already hard at work. Antonio went to his office to prioritize his 'to-do' list. After a short time, Sandra came in.

"Mr. Petrocelli, there's someone from the district here to see you."

"Thanks Sandra." Sandra ushered in a middle-aged man wearing a gray pin-striped suit. His silver hair was neat and smelled like he'd just come from Super Cuts.

"Hello, Mr. Petrocelli. I'm Mr. Magnus from Human Resources." He shook Antonio's hand and took a seat. "As you know, we have an opening to fill due to Mrs. Roger's death. What a tragedy. She was a lovely woman."

"Yes, we all miss her." Antonio felt his pulse quicken.

"Mr. Ford already has a critical role as the assistant principal here and is doing an excellent job. He has no desire to assume the extra duties involved in taking over the principal job. He shared with me that he plans to retire next year. We don't want to fix what isn't broken, so the board has decided that we should respect his wishes and leave him in his current position. We'd like to offer you the Principal position. We know that you already know the ropes here at Westbrook and we feel it would be an easy transition."

"Thank you, I'm flattered." Antonio knew that his dimples were showing.

"So, is that a yes?" asked Mr. Magnus?

"Of course, it's a yes. I'm fully committed to Westbrook and I won't let you down." Antonio took a deep breath in hopes that he could slow down his racing heartbeat.

"Great. I'll have a contract prepared and will send it over shortly."

"Thank you, Mr. Magnus. And please express my appreciation to the board." Antonio felt like he wanted to cartwheel across the office. Finally his dream had come true. He couldn't wait to tell Hayley.

Chapter 20

Jackson and Lynette drove to the apartment complex where Blaze had supposedly been the night of the murder. The exterior of the three-story buildings had been newly painted pale yellow. They drove by a basketball court and a swimming pool which was covered tightly for the winter. Lynette noticed a small building next to the pool.

"Let's park here." The lot was flanked with pine trees. "This looks like the rental office. Hopefully someone will be there," said Lynette. She pulled the picture of Blaze out from her briefcase. They entered the small building which housed both a clubhouse and a rental area. A portly older gentleman sat behind the desk eating an Italian hero sandwich.

"Good evening, sir. We're from the Westbrook Police Department. I'm Jackson Simpson and this is my partner."

Lynette extended her hand and introduced herself. "We need your help. We're investigating a recent homicide. We were wondering if you recognize this man," asked Lynette. She handed him the photo.

"Let me take a look." He took the photo from Lynette. "Sure. He comes around here a lot. He visits Miss Barbie Doll up there on the second floor." The manager pointed out the door and upwards. Then he took another bite of his sandwich, dripping Italian dressing onto the wax paper wrapper.

"Think back. Can you remember seeing him specifically on the evening of December 17th?" asked Lynette.

"Do I look like Rain Man? I have no idea if I saw him that day or not," said the manager.

"Well, then, do you keep some type of log or do you have surveillance videos?" asked Lynette.

"I guess this is your lucky day," replied the manager. "We do have security videos. Don't you need a warrant for those?" There was an awkward silence. Neither Jackson nor Lynette even cracked a smile. "Just kidding. I'll go get them." He returned several minutes later with a DVD labeled *December* which he handed to Lynette.

"Thank you for your help," said Lynette. She and Jackson took the DVD and left the building.

"I really hope this gives us the information we need," said Lynette. Next, she and Jackson walked across to the apartment building where the lady with the poodle lived. They climbed the steps to her apartment.

They knocked and heard a dog barking maniacally. "That's why I prefer cats," said Lynette. A gray-haired elderly Italian woman wearing a flowered housecoat opened the door.

"Hello, ma'am." Jackson flashed his badge. "How are you doing today?"

"I'm fine. What can I do for you?"

"We're hoping you can help us. We are with the Westbrook Police Department. We're investigating a murder. Would you mind taking a look at this photo? Have you by any chance seen this man?" Jackson handed the photo to the lady. She put on her reading glasses which she wore dangling from a beaded chain around her neck.

"Yes, he's around here quite often. He's usually with Miss Pratt, the blonde lady who lives next door."

"Would you possibly remember if you saw him here the night of December 17? I know it's hard to remember a specific date. It was a Monday night," asked Lynette.

"Why yes I do. That happens to be my grandson's birthday. I was carrying in a cake and a bag of groceries. Marybeth, Miss Pratt, and I talked about how we used to enjoy baking birthday cakes but with the fabulous bakery section at Safeway it's more convenient and probably cheaper to buy them. I had bought chips and dip, baby carrots, soda. He and Marybeth were nice enough to help me carry them to my door. Later that night, I saw them again when I was walking Fritzie."

"Thank you, ma'am. You've been extremely helpful," said Jackson.

"Anytime," said the woman. Lynette could have sworn the woman was flirting with Jackson. *She must be* very *lonely,* thought Lynette.

Lynette and Jackson drove back to the station.

"I'll go through the surveillance tapes and you keep working on locating Dr. Manning," said Lynette. She thumbed through the stack of DVDs and quickly located the week in question. She popped it into the machine and *voila.* "There he is," said Lynette. The tape was date and time stamped. "There's no way Blaze Conrad could have killed Vicky."

"Wow, this gives him an alibi," said Jackson. "Well, then, let's focus on Javier. I just pulled up the doctor's address. I also went through his credit card records and have a hit. We can check that location. It appears to be en route to the address I found for Dr. Manning."

"Wait, Jackson, not so fast. Look at this."

"That's the girlfriend leaving her apartment alone," said Jackson.

"And what's she carrying?" asked Lynette

"It's a small Tupperware container," answered Jackson.

"She seemed to have a stake in Ryan's well being. And she's quite protective of Blaze," said Lynette. Lynette couldn't help remembering the information her mother had shared with her on Christmas Day. She hated when her mom's snooping actually panned out. Certainly she didn't want to encourage her.

"It's a bit of a long shot but we should look into this," said Jackson.

"Well, that will take some time," said Lynette. "Right now we need to follow up on Javier. Let's go. I'll grab my purse."

"I can't. I have a dentist appointment. I cracked a tooth this morning on a piece of stale bagel. She's squeezing me in. We can go in the morning."

"Fine," said Lynette. She couldn't help being disappointed. She felt like they were close to a big break. She grabbed her coat and purse and went out to her car to go home. The sun was low in the sky and Lynette could feel the drop in temperature. She turned the key….nothing. It wouldn't even start, not a whimper, not a sputter….nothing. She kicked the front tire. *Now what?* she thought. *I'm so sick of this old car.* Jason was teaching a class so she knew he couldn't come to her rescue. *I guess I'll have to get mom to pick me up…again.* She called and Susan was happy to help. Like always, her mom was there for her. She arrived a short time later.

Chapter 21

"Hey, you and Jason really need to replace that heap," said Susan, pointing to Lynette's car. "Maybe you could look into one of those certified pre-owned ones. They're much less expensive than new ones and they have a warranty. The lady who does my nails just bought one and she's thrilled with it. It's a cute, blue Camry. I saw it parked outside the salon. It looks brand new."

Lynette seemed distracted.

"What else is wrong? I can tell your mood is about more than the car," said Susan

Lynette hesitated. "I really wanted to follow a lead we had but Jackson had to leave for a dentist appointment so it'll have to wait till morning. We think we may know where Javier was headed."

"I'll drive," offered Susan. Lynette could swear that her Mom's eyes brightened. She also detected a hint of excitement in her mom's voice.

"You know I can't take you on official business," said Lynette.

"Well, couldn't it be unofficial? Just a mom and her daughter taking a little ride through the country."

Lynette thought for a moment. If she didn't have such a strong hunch about this she would have said no, but instead she said, "Okay, but we'll just go look. Nothing official."

First, Lynette checked the location where they'd gotten a hit on Javier's credit card. It was a Shell Station just off the highway, about an hour out of town.

"We need to get on the Thruway," said Lynette.

"No problem." Susan got on the Thruway.

Bringing her mom along on police business was against Lynnette's better judgment, but she was too anxious to wait until tomorrow.

"It's the next exit," said Lynette. "It's coming up soon."

When they got to the gas station, they got out of the car and walked into the dilapidated Mini-Mart. Lynette pulled her scarf closer around her neck. When they went inside, Lynette noticed that the white tile floor was filthy and the donuts under the glass case looked as if they'd been there since the days of the dinosaurs. She walked over to the cashier and showed him Javier's picture.

"Do you remember seeing this man around Christmas Day?" asked Lynette.

"I wasn't working on Christmas," said the cashier. "Let me get my manager. He's always here."

Soon a young man wearing blue Dockers and a white button down shirt came out from behind the glass. "Can I help you?"

"I'm from the Westbrook Police Department." Lynette showed him Javier's picture. "Do you remember seeing this man recently?"

The manager looked at the picture. "I do. I only remember because he was the only one who stopped in all night. It was Christmas night. He got gas and a few snacks."

"Did he happen to say where he was headed? Think hard. Could you tell whether or not he'd been drinking?"

"Well, I didn't get into a conversation with him," said the manager. "He seemed to be in a hurry. He seemed perfectly sober to me though."

"Thanks," said Lynette. "We appreciate the info." Although this was not official business, Lynette was still wearing her uniform. She couldn't help it if people assumed they had to talk to her, right?

"Okay, Mom. If we keep going on this road we'll get to the address we have for Dr. Manning. Are you game?"

"You bet," said Susan. Lynette could hear the excitement in her voice.

They got back on the windy mountain road. By now it was getting dark.

"It's kind of hard to see, even with my brights on,"

"I can drive, Mom."

"No, it's okay. Maybe on the way home I'll take you up on that though."

Evergreens lined both sides of the road which was punctuated with 'deer crossing' and 'fallen rock zone' signs. After driving another hour, the road forked. They could continue going straight, or turn right onto a one lane dirt road.

"This reminds me of the poem by Robert Frost. Which way should I go?" asked Susan.

"According to the address we have, we should go straight," replied Lynette.

The road narrowed significantly and the sound of rocks crunching as they continued reminded Lynette that they were pretty much in the middle of nowhere. *She never should have dragged her mother out here*, she thought. They continued up a mountain for what seemed like an eternity. Finally there was a sign.

"Can you see what that says?" asked Susan.

Lynette's body relaxed as she read the sign. It was not at all what she expected. The rustic wooden sign was painted in yellow letters. It read, *Shady Oaks Alcoholic Rehab Center*.

Chapter 22

"Oh my," said Susan. This isn't what I expected. "Let's go in."

"Okay, Mom," said Lynette, "But remember, this is not official police business. We'll just get a feel for the place and find out if Javier here. Let's park in the visitor's lot."

There were only a few cars in the parking lot. They went inside and Lynette checked the sign on the interior wall which listed doctors and their office numbers.

"Look, there's our Dr. Manning; his office is on the third floor," said Lynette. They approached the front desk.

"Excuse me; I'm with the Westbrook Police Department. I was wondering if we could speak with Dr. Manning?" asked Lynette.

The friendly brunette at the desk answered, "I'm sorry, but he's gone home for the evening. Office hours are long over and he already made his rounds."

"Well," said Lynette, "Can you check and see if there's a patient here by the name of Javier Rogers:" She knew this violated all the privacy laws but she was hoping that her uniform would be her trump card. It was.

"Yes, he's here. He's in room 410."

"Thanks. May we still visit?" asked Lynette.

"Yes, visiting hours end in twenty minutes. Please sign here and here are your visitor badges. The elevator is around the corner."

"Thank you. You've been very helpful," said Lynette.

Lynette and Susan rode the elevator to the 4th floor where they found Javier's room. He was wearing a flannel bathrobe and watching TV.

"Good evening, Mr. Rogers. I'm Lynette Sanders and this is my mom Susan Wiles. We'd like to ask you a few questions."

"I was Carolina's music teacher and worked for Vicky. Carolina has been so worried about you. We told her we'd try to make sure you were safe."

"Carolina, *mi hija*. I love her so much. That's why I came here. I was such a poor example for her. I lost my job, I drank too much, and my relationship with her mother was falling apart. I am going to turn my life around for my daughter. I'm going to do whatever it takes to get sober. I've started working through the twelve steps. Then I'll go back, find a job, and be a father to her." Lynette noticed a tear on his cheek.

"I have to ask," said Lynette. "Did you have anything to do with your wife's death?"

"No, of course not; I didn't kill her."

"We have a receipt showing you were near the school the night she was killed," said Lynette. "And we know you'd just been served divorce papers. Oh, and then there was the restraining order..."

"Yes, you are right. I did go to the school that night. I was furious. I waited in her office until intermission. When she came in, I screamed at her. Then I begged her to give it another try. She laughed at me. Called me a first class loser. She said she wished she'd never met me."

"And then..."

"Then I lost my temper and punched her right in the face. I know that was wrong but I just exploded."

"Why didn't you call for help then?" asked Lynette.

"Oh, her face was red but that didn't stop her from humiliating me some more and threatening to call the cops. Besides, I was violating the restraining order. I just left. Ran away like a coward."

"And you're saying she was alive when you left?" asked Lynette.

"Of course, she was. It would have taken more than a punch from me to defeat her," said Javier.

"Thank you for talking to us," said Lynnette. "Good luck with your recovery."

"Bye," said Susan. "I'm so happy that I can tell Carolina that you are safe and getting help. She will be thrilled. She loves you very much."

"Tell her I love her too and hope I can see her soon."

When they were back in the car, Susan asked, "Do you believe him? Do you still think he killed Vicky?"

"I don't know, but I got the sense he was telling us the truth. And it always bothered me—the amount of bruising she had doesn't seem like enough to have killed her. I still need the medical examiner's report. It's taking ridiculously long since the ME took a little Christmas break himself."

"I'm thinking it could still be one of those cryptic contacts on the secret cell phone we found. Maybe we should look into those?" said Susan.

"Again, Mom, I know how to do my job. And it's not *we*. Jackson and I will explore all possibilities."

Susan called Carolina from the car to tell her what they'd learned while Lynette drove them back home. By now Jason would be home and he could pick her up at her mom's house.

Chapter 23

By the next morning, the medical examiner was back at work. By mid afternoon he had confirmed that the blows to Vicky's face were not forceful enough to have been lethal.

"Jackson, look at this report," said Lynette. She handed him the manila file.

"Well, Javier was telling the truth. The blows she suffered weren't hard enough to kill Vicky. And look at this. Vicky was in perfect health—except for being dead. The report rules out heart attack or stroke. And there were no signs of an aneurysm. Look at this though." Lynette flipped over the page and pointed to a section of the report."

"Well, this changes the game. Not only was she murdered, but it had to have been premeditated," said Jackson.

Just then an elderly woman with wire-rimmed glasses came through the door.

"Excuse me, officers, but I need to file a police report. I just had my purse snatched while I was pushing my grocery cart to the car. I should have accepted that young boy's offer to help me out with the groceries but even though it's against store policy, I always feel guilty not tipping the baggers when they help you to your car." The woman looked stressed. Her hair was mussed and there was sweat on her brow despite the cold temperature.

"I'll help you out with that," offered Jackson. Lynette hated paperwork but Jackson almost seemed to enjoy it. Plus, he made far fewer errors.

The new information gleaned between last night and today changes the course of this investigation dramatically, thought Lynette. Her phone vibrated. It was Jason.

"Hey, Hon, come on down so we can get to the repair shop."

"I'll be right out." She straightened the top of her desk and grabbed her purse and jacket. She was hoping this wasn't going to be an overly expensive repair. The mechanic had given them quite a price range as an estimate. Of course, he wouldn't know until he dismantled half the car what the exact problem was. How did that always seem to be the scenario? Didn't they hook up cars to a computer these days to diagnose these things?

Lynette got into Jason's car and they drove to the repair shop. She could find it blindfolded by now considering how many times they'd brought her car in.

"Well, it's not as bad as I thought," said Jason. Lynette had waited in the car while Jason attended to the paperwork. "That car of yours has nine lives."

"And I think we're at least at number eight," said Lynette. *How nice would it be to trade in this heap for a nice new car—one that smelled like leather and had voice controls and Pandora.* She got out, reclaimed her car, and drove to Coppola's to meet her mom for dinner like she did nearly every Thursday night. Jason taught class on Thursday nights and Mike had a standing poker game with his buddies. Her mom was already seated when she arrived.

"But that's nearly impossible," said Susan, putting her spoon down in her minestrone. "Westbrook has been a peanut-free school for at least five years now.

There's no way there could have been peanuts in that cupcake."

"That's what the lab report said," said Lynette. "I had them check it twice. And the medical examiner found evidence of swelling in her throat as well as hives under that suit she was wearing. Why wasn't she wearing a medic alert bracelet? I didn't know she was allergic to peanuts until I read it in the coroner's report. She died from anaphylactic shock."

Lynette gulped her beer. *Why not drink since yet another month had gone by without conceiving?* she thought. She and Jason had been trying to have a baby for well over a year now. She hoped her Mom wouldn't ask about it since it just made her feel more anxious and upset.

"She said those medic alert bracelets clashed with her wardrobe." said Susan. "You know what a meticulous dresser she was. Besides, everyone already knew. Remember I told you how Hayley baked those delicious mock peanut butter cookies for the holiday party? And come on, Westbrook has a reputation for being peanut-free. *Sixty Minutes* even did a feature on us." Susan took a sip of her Diet Coke.

"I knew about the school, but even so, if Vicky was so allergic, shouldn't she have carried an Epi-pen with her?" Lynette wiped her garlicky hands on her napkin.

"I'm sure she did. I heard her telling a parent whose child had the same allergy that she carried one in her purse, stashed one in her desk drawer, and had several in her house." She dipped the tines of her fork into the salad dressing and stabbed a chunk of cucumber. "This is a calorie-saving trick I heard on *The Doctors*," said Susan. Lynette ignored the comment.

"We didn't find one anywhere in her office. And her purse was nowhere to be found." Lynette took a bite of her Creamy Italian drenched salad. "Even stranger, the cupcake didn't come from the bake sale. I questioned the moms who were running it the night of the concert. No one remembered funfetti cupcakes, only red velvet ones with red or green frosting. And certainly Vicky didn't bring along a peanut-laden cupcake to have as a snack."

The young waitress set their entrees on the table. For Lynette, fettuccini alfredo with a side of sausage. Susan ordered angel hair cappelini with a to-go box. For as long as Lynette could remember, her mom always asked for a to-go box at the beginning of a meal so that she could pack away half the calories before she started eating. *Good thing I inherited Dad's metabolism,* thought Lynette. *Having to keep track of every bite would drive me crazy.*

"Are you saying it was deliberate?" asked Susan.

"It's looking that way," said Lynette. She could hear the enthusiasm in her mom's voice. *There was something a little sick about getting excited over a murder,* she thought. Then again, she'd chosen to spend her own life solving murders. She supposed the apple didn't fall far from the tree.

"What about investigating the men Vicky had in the contacts list?" said Susan

"I already told you we'd look into it, but we don't have much to go on. We'll investigate all the avenues. Relax, Mom."

Chapter 24

"Well, if you paid better attention to your son's needs he wouldn't need to curse at the teacher and attack his classmates. A fifth-grader biting another student? Get out of here. They should require a license to have children," screamed Jody. She stood up from her desk.

"You're going to hear from my lawyer. How dare you talk to me like this? My taxes pay your salary." The irate father stormed out of Jody's office. Jody took the opportunity to slam the door behind him. She took a deep breath and counted to ten. Antonio came running in.

"Are you okay? What happened with that parent?"

"Just another case of a parent turning a blind eye to his child's issues. I'm fine. I do want him to be suspended for the week though. At least his teacher and classmates will get a break."

"I'm on it," said Antonio. Antonio had seamlessly taken over the role of principal. His faculty respected him and accepted his authority. The parents, for the most part, were relieved to see that the school was moving past the tragedy of Vicky's murder.

"We're having a little party at the house Saturday night to celebrate my promotion. I hope you can make it," said Antonio.

"That sounds like fun," said Jody. "I'll be there. Can I bring anything?"

"No, Hayley has it covered but thanks." Antonio strutted back to his office. A few minutes later, Theresa came in with her lunch.

"Hey, ready for lunch?" said Theresa.

"Sure, I could use a break." Jody took a sandwich out of her mini fridge.

"I'm glad they canceled the faculty meeting. I'm exhausted and just want to get home early today," said Theresa.

"I hear you. I'm pretty tired myself after dealing with that crazy parent." Jody opened her desk drawer. "Here, have some chocolate."

"Thanks. So, are you going to the party Saturday night?" Theresa ate the chocolate and then took a yogurt out of her lunch box. "I hear that house of theirs is really something. It'll be worth going just to check it out."

"Sure. I'll pick you up on the way. A new principal is certainly a reason to celebrate."

Chapter 25

Hayley had finally gotten the baby down for a nap. She dusted the living room furniture and took out the vacuum. There was a lot of work to do before Saturday. Next, she went into the study and dumped the wastebasket. *There's so much clutter in here,* she thought. *I wish Antonio could be a little more organized.* She seldom came in here but with the party on the horizon she wanted the whole house to be in shape just in case anyone wandered in here. She straightened up the papers on the desk, but was still dissatisfied. *Let me see if I can stuff these in a drawer* she thought. She opened the first drawer but it was too tightly packed. Then she opened the middle drawer. This one had potential. She pulled out the folders that were already in there. If she consolidated some of this junk maybe there would be room. She opened the first folder and threw away the papers that were obviously trash. She opened the second folder and began leafing through its contents. There were drawings that Tony had made, a birthday card she'd given him a few months ago, and...another card. This one didn't look like something she'd have chosen. It had a cartoon of a busty waitress on the front carrying a tray with a stack of syrup covered pancakes. Inside it said, "want some sugar?" It was written to *boy toy* and signed *Love, Vicky. Just confirms what I already knew,* thought Hayley. *It's okay though. He's definitely going to pay for this.*

Chapter 26

Susan used the funky scissors to cut around a photo taken last summer on their anniversary cruise. To some people, a cruise was as mundane as going out to dinner, but to her and Mike it was a big deal. They'd saved all year for it and Mike had secured his vacation time months in advance. It had been wonderful. They flew to Miami and cruised around the Bahamas for a whole week. Susan had never been on a cruise before. How unusual was that, to find a woman in her sixties who had never been on a cruise before? She was a little afraid of getting seasick but she never even had to use the acupressure bracelet or the ear patch she'd packed. Here was a photo of them with the trophy they won playing the on-board version of *The Dating Game*. She pasted it on a turquoise square of construction paper and then arranged it on a nautical-themed scrapbook page. *Boy, this is tedious*, she thought. She'd been working for hours and just now finished one page.

Her mind wandered back to Vicky's murder. *Hmmm*, she thought. *I still wonder about those contacts on Vicky's secret cell phone*. Maybe someone who worked at the Omni would remember seeing Vicky with someone. The Hilton wasn't far from there either. She knew it was definitely a long shot. And what would I get from that? It's possible, though not probable, that she could find out the identity of *boy toy* or *macho man*. Perhaps one of them had a good reason for wanting to kill Vicky. Anyone could have come in and put that cupcake on her desk. Anyone who'd spent any time with her at all would have known about her severe peanut allergy. The school was open the night of the concert. Susan evaluated staying home and finishing another page of her scrapbook, against going into the city for a little investigating. She could get lunch there and do a little shopping. There wasn't much traffic on a weekday and she'd be home before Mike got back from work. Okay, she'd talked herself into it. She fed Johann and Ludwig, then changed into a pair of black pants and a cashmere sweater. It felt nice to put on real clothes and do her makeup. Most days she lived in sweats and yoga pants.

Susan hopped into her blue Prius and entered the address of the Omni into the GPS, patting herself on the back for knowing how to do this. It was a beautiful, clear day. The sky was as blue as a robin's egg, the air was crisp and dry, and the sun made the snow glisten. It was her favorite kind of winter day. She turned on the radio. They were playing a *Maroon 5* song. Adam Levine was a far cry from Pavarotti but she enjoyed his songs. An hour later, she pulled in front of the Omni. Sunlight reflected off the glass skyscraper. She gave the valet her key and walked through the ornate lobby doors. *Wow, this place is beautiful,* she thought. The floor was marble and the walls were decorated with colorful modern artwork. Black leather sofas and love seats formed a conversion pit in the center of the lobby. She walked up to the front desk.

"Can I help you?" said the woman behind the desk.

"Good morning, I was wondering if you remember seeing this woman. I dropped my wallet right in front of your hotel a few weeks ago and she picked it up and returned it to me. You know, that's unusual for city people. Anyhow, I had taken a photo of your beautiful lobby doors and, low and behold, when I went home and saw the pictures, she was in that one. I know I thanked her already, but when I got home I was thinking maybe I should have offered her a little reward."

Susan held her breath. She showed her the picture on her phone. It was actually from one of Susan's concerts. "I guess I dropped my wallet while taking out my camera." Susan surprised herself with how elaborate her lie was. She hoped it would be believable.

"No, I'm sorry I don't recognize her," said the uniformed 'customer welfare specialist.' That was her actual title. Susan was surprised that whole thing could fit on a badge.

"Thanks, anyway." Susan decided to try the 'uniformed room hygiene specialists.' She took the elevator to the tenth floor. *Even the elevators are ornate,* thought Susan. She brushed her hair in the mirror, feeling suddenly self conscious. Susan worked her way down, showing Vicky's picture to any of the cleaning women, bell hops, and room service workers she saw in the hallway. No one remembered seeing her. Susan couldn't help feeling disappointed even though she knew coming into this that it would be a long shot.

Susan got back into the car and tried the same routine at the Hilton. The lobby was less ornate than the one at the Omni, but it was impressive none the less. She tried the restaurant first. This time she hit pay dirt. The waitress in the café remembered seeing Vicky.

"Yes, she came in here a few times with a handsome, dark haired guy. He had these great dimples—a real charmer." The waitress handed the phone back to Susan.

Dimples, thought Susan. *Handsome? Dark haired?* She scrolled through her photos and found another concert picture. This one had Antonio in it.

"Was this the man you saw by any chance?" asked Susan.

"Yes, I'm pretty sure that's him."

Now she knew Antonio was either *boy toy* or *macho man*. Susan wasn't sure how this information would be helpful but she had a hunch it would be. She had to figure out a way to relay this new info to Lynette without getting a lecture about snooping.

"Thank you," she told the waitress. It was long past lunch time and Susan was starving. After enjoying a spinach salad and French onion soup, she left a generous tip and headed back home.

Chapter 27

Antonio and Hayley lived in an upscale neighborhood in the newer part of town. On Saturday night, Susan and Mike arrived at the Portcullis house carrying a platter of cut vegetables and artichoke dip. Susan's emerald green dress complimented her stylish blond hair. Mike wore a striped dress shirt and gray slacks. The invitation said semiformal dress which Susan knew he'd interpreted as not having to wear a tie. His wavy brown hair had just been cut and Susan could smell a hint of aftershave. She loved how he looked when he was dressed up. Mike knocked on the cherry wood door.

"Come in. So glad you're here," said Hayley.

"This house is beautiful," said Susan.

"Thanks. We really worked with the builder to get it just the way we wanted it. We had the fireplace moved from the living room to the den." Hayley pointed to a door on the other side of the living room. "We added a Jacuzzi and a walk-in closet to the bedroom, and we upgraded to granite countertops in the kitchen. I'll have to give you the tour later."

"Well, it looks lovely," said Susan. "I hope you enjoy many happy years here."

Hayley looked gorgeous in a low-cut silver dress. Her hair was sculpted into an up-do. She took their coats and ushered them into the living room. Susan put the vegetable platter on the table which was filled with miniature quiches, egg rolls, Swedish meatballs, and bacon-wrapped scallops. Classical music played softly in the background.

"What can I get you to drink?" she asked

"I'll take a glass of white wine," answered Susan.

"I'll have the same," answered Mike.

Susan was glad he was savvy enough not to ask for a beer. Somehow, beer just didn't go well with canapés and bacon wrapped scallops.

"Hi, I'm Margaux. I'm Hayley's mom," said a classy-looking woman in a black cocktail dress. Susan thought the designer dress a bit over the top for semi-formal. She extended her hand. Susan could definitely see the family resemblance, especially around the chin area.

"I'm Susan and this is my husband Mike. I worked with Antonio."

"Glad to meet you. I'm so happy that Antonio finally got a principal job. No one can support a family on a teaching salary."

Susan was thinking that you indeed could if you could live without up-dos and granite countertops, but she refrained from voicing her opinion. Just then Theresa and Jody arrived.

"What an incredible spread," said Jody. "And this house is gorgeous." They assembled heaping plates of food and came into the living room.

"Hi, Susan. You look great. We miss you at school. My kids don't come back from music as excited as they did last year. They miss you," said Theresa. She sat on the leather couch next to Susan.

"Thanks for telling me that," said Susan. "I miss them too, although I can't say I'm not enjoying all the free time I have now." *I've lots of time to paste pictures into scrapbooks and organize the refrigerator*, thought Susan. *How did I ever survive having the mayonnaise thrown into the crisper drawer?*

"You're lucky you're gone," said Jody. "Kids today are crazier every year. Their parents are too. I wish these parents weren't so clueless. If it's your kid you should know if they are heading into problems, don't you think?" She took a bite of her egg roll.

"Yes, I saw a lot of changes in the years I taught. When I first started teaching most of the kids wouldn't dare talk back to a teacher or a parent. There'd be maybe one bad seed in the bunch. It's all technology's fault. They just play those video games and text all day long," said Susan.

"I think it's because families don't eat dinner together anymore," added Theresa.

Antonio came over in the middle of this conversation.

"Don't worry, I'm cleaning up the behavior now that I'm in charge." Antonio chuckled but Susan knew there was some truth in that. Or, at least Antonio believed it was true.

"I'd like to propose a toast." Hayley's father clinked a fork against his champagne glass. He was tall and handsome with the same dimples that Antonio had. Hayley had hired a helper for the party. She came around with a tray of champagne. "To Antonio and his new position. I knew it would happen eventually." Glasses were raised and the guests drank to Westbrook Elementary's new principal.

"Come get some dinner," said Hayley. The appetizers had been replaced with trays of lasagna and carved ham. There were dinner rolls still warm from the oven, and the butter was shaped into little rosebuds. Susan and Mike helped themselves and sat down at a folding table covered with a linen tablecloth.

"This is delicious," said Mike. "I haven't had ham in a while."

"It sure is. I love this lasagna. You know me and Italian food; we've had a love affair all my life," said Susan.

Jody and Theresa set down their plates and had seats at the table with Susan and Mike. "These rolls taste like they just came out of the oven," said Theresa. They cleaned their plates while conversing. All four of them went back for seconds.

"Excuse me, but I need the ladies room," said Susan. She rose from the table and felt how full she was. "I'll be back in a minute." Susan tried the bathroom door but it was locked.

Hayley walked by. "There's another bathroom in our bedroom," said Hayley. It's just at the top of the stairs on the right."

Susan found the bedroom without a problem, but when she opened what she thought was the bathroom door, it turned out to be a walk in closet. She flicked the light on. *It's at least as big as a bathroom*, thought Susan. She couldn't help rifling through the clothes on Hayley's side of the closet. Hayley had impeccable taste. Lynette would have called this snooping, but really it was just research. Who knew when she would have a fancy banquet to attend? Suddenly something gold and sparkly caught her eye. On the floor, behind the clothes, was a gold sequined purse. It looked familiar but Susan didn't think it was Hayley's. This was a little gaudy for Hayley's taste. Besides, Hayley always carried a fabric bag. Susan had even ordered a Vera Bradley diaper bag for Hayley's baby shower because she'd heard Hayley mention loving that designer on more than one occasion. *I wonder what that's doing here?* She knew it was wrong to keep snooping but she couldn't help it. She unclasped the purse. Inside was a leather wallet. It still smelled new. Susan found Vicky's driver's license and credit cards inside. *Oh, my God*! she thought. This means that either Hayley or Antonio killed Vicky. She found an Epi-pen in the purse as well. *This would have saved her,* she thought. Either Hayley or Antonio was so cold-blooded that they'd put peanuts in the cupcake and then made sure Vicky would die from anaphylactic shock.

Which one, though? Antonio benefited from Vicky's death because he got her job. It was difficult to come by a principal job in Westbrook. And he was having an affair with her. Maybe she threatened to tell Hayley. Then again, maybe Hayley found out about the affair and took it out on Vicky. Hayley could be very calculating. She could picture her executing such an elaborate plan. *I'm sure she hasn't been getting a lot of sleep with a new baby.* Maybe she even has post-partum depression. Maybe she snapped from exhaustion. And she did enjoy baking. *Her chocolate brownies were to die for. Oops, that was not a good choice of words,* thought Susan. It was impossible to determine which of the Petrocellis had stashed the purse here.

Susan suddenly heard voices in the hallway and quickly thought to close the closet door and turn off the light. How embarrassing would it be to be caught in here? She held her breath and her heart was pounding. Oh no, now I'm sweating in my good dress. She hoped she wasn't in the process of creating underarm stains but then she remembered she had bigger issues. Someone was coming into the bedroom. She heard talking.

"Oh, here it is. I must have left it in here. The doctor said to use it with every diaper change because the baby's rash was pretty bad." Susan recognized Hayley's voice and hoped she didn't remember having sent her in here to the bathroom. "No problem. I'll take care of him," Susan recognized the young voice as that of the hired helper. Then she heard the bedroom door close and it was quiet again. Susan let out her breath. She gently opened the closet door, went down the stairs and rejoined the party.

Chapter 28

"But, Mike, there's no plausible explanation as to why Vicky's purse was in the closet. Either Hayley or Antonio has to be responsible for Vicky's murder."

"There you go with your overactive imagination again. Maybe it wasn't even Vicky's purse," said Mike.

"Then why were Vicky's wallet and Epi-pen inside?" asked Susan.

"Well, maybe Vicky *borrowed* the purse from Hayley and returned it, forgetting her things were still inside."

"Now who has an overactive imagination? Vicky would have checked inside before returning it," said Susan.

"Let's get some sleep. You can discuss this with Lynette in the morning." Mike nudged Ludwig off the bedspread and climbed under the covers.

Susan was anxious to tell Lynette, even though it meant admitting she'd been snooping. It wasn't intentional snooping though. It truly was an accident, or maybe karma, that she wound up in that closet. Finding out that Antonio was in all likelihood *boy toy* or *macho man* by driving to the Omni and the Hilton and showing Vicky's picture around under false pretenses–that was a different story.

She tossed and turned all night long. The blue walls weren't helping tonight. What if Westbrook Elementary was being led by a cold blooded killer? It was bad enough that he was a cheater. Poor Hayley—pregnant with his child, holding things together at home while her husband was out gallivanting. Susan got out of bed and turned down the temperature. Maybe that would help her fall asleep. 2am, 3am....the red light of the clock radio was a constant source of stress, reminding her of how few hours of sleep she was getting. Thank God she didn't have to go to work in the morning. Maybe she should ask her doctor about a prescription for Ambien in case this happened again. Her friend Maggie swore by it. No, maybe that wasn't such a great idea. She remembered seeing a segment on Dr. Phil about this lady who took Ambien and started cooking and eating pasta in the middle of the night. She kept gaining weight and didn't understand why because she had no recollection of doing this. Her husband was going to leave her because he thought she'd become a prescription pill addict, and because she'd gained thirty pounds. Dr. Phil had to patch things up for them. Susan decided to make herself a cup of chamomile tea.

Susan was relieved to see the first hint of sunlight through the window.

"Lynette, I have some important information for you." Susan called Lynette's cell even before getting out of bed. Mike was still sound asleep beside her. "I found Vicky's purse in Antonio and Hayley's closet last night. Don't ask. I think you need to go over there and get it. The Epi-pen was still in it."

"Vicky's purse in Hayley's closet. How much sleep did you get last night, Mom?"

"I'm serious. This is really important."

"What on earth were you doing in her closet?" asked Lynette.

"I was looking for the restroom. That house is so big, I'm sure I'm not the first person to have gotten lost in there," said Susan.

"Uh huh. We'll go with that," said Lynette. "How do you even know it was Vicky's?"

"I checked the wallet," said Susan.

"This really sounds crazy, Mom," said Lynette. "I wish you would just keep your nose out of trouble."

"But Lynette…this is an important clue. You should be thanking me for this information."

"Yeah, okay, Mom. I'll check it out. It's Sunday so it might take a while to get a search warrant. "

"I have one more piece of information for you. I don't want any lectures about snooping though," said Susan

"Just tell me."

"I took a little ride to the Omni and the Hilton the other day. The waitress at the Hilton recognized Vicky and Antonio and remembered seeing them together on a few occasions. I'll bet he's one of the cryptic contacts that were on Vicky's phone."

"Mom, I told you Jackson and I are going to look into that. You have to be patient. Just because Vicky and Antonio were involved with each other doesn't mean he killed her."

"I know, but it could be a piece of the puzzle," said Susan.

"But this isn't your puzzle, Mom. Let me go and get busy securing a warrant. Go work on your scrapbook. I'll talk to you later," said Lynette.

Chapter 29

It had taken several hours, but Lynette had the search warrant in hand.

"Come on, let's get over to the Petrocelli household," said Lynette. Jackson followed her into the cruiser. He looked like a bird that had just swallowed a canary.

"Okay, Jackson. I know you're dying to tell me something."

"I called Theresa Rizzo last night," said Jackson.

"Wow, I'm proud of you. What did you say?"

"I told her I thought she was really pretty and nice and I wanted to go out with her," said Jackson.

"That sounds a little sketchy," said Lynette.

"I guess it was. She said she was really busy with work right now but maybe sometime. Sounds like a blow off to me," said Jackson.

"Well, don't lose hope. Next time we'll do a little role playing before you call."

Jackson raised his eyebrows and tilted his head.

"Relax. Not that kind of role playing," said Lynette.

Just then, they pulled into Antonio's driveway. Jackson knocked on the door.

"Can I help you?" Antonio answered the door wearing a thermal undershirt and pajama bottoms. He had yet to comb his hair. "What can I do for you, officers?"

"Good morning, Sir. Sorry to bother you so early in the morning but we have a warrant to search your premises," said Jackson.

Antonio unfolded the paper, rubbed his eyes, and read it. Twice."

"Please get your family together and wait here in the living room," said Lynette.

Antonio looked thoroughly puzzled. "A search warrant? For our house?"

"Yes, Sir. We'll start upstairs," said Lynette.

Just then, Hayley entered the living room wearing a satin robe and carrying the baby. Tony followed behind her like a baby duckling.

"What's this about?" she asked.

"They have a search warrant," said Antonio. "I can't imagine what they'd be looking for." They sat on the sofa. "This is totally insane. They'll realize that when they don't find anything. Let them waste their time."

Jackson and Lynette headed up the stairs. "This way, Jackson. Mom said the purse was in the closet in the master bedroom."

"And your mom knows that because…"

"Never mind. In here." Lynette led him to the closet and turned on the light. Sure enough, there was a gold purse on the floor. Lynette put on gloves, although she knew this evidence had already been compromised. She would most likely have to explain how her mom's prints got on the purse. Lynette opened it and took out the wallet. Sure enough, there was Vicky's driver's license and credit cards. It was Vicky's.

"Now what?" asked Jackson.

"I think we should continue with a thorough search," said Lynette. "Let's go through the rest of the bedroom. I'll check under the bed. Why don't you check the dresser drawers?"

Jackson carefully emptied each of the dresser drawers.

"Nothing unusual here," he said.

"Nothing under the bed either, except for a few match box cars. Let's check the other upstairs rooms and then go downstairs into the study," said Lynette. They searched through Tony's room, the baby's room, and the guest room but found nothing alarming. *The baby's room is adorable*, thought Lynette. *If I ever do have a baby, I'll borrow that idea of painting a forest mural on the wall opposite the crib.*

"I didn't find anything unusual up here," said Jackson. "Why don't we try downstairs?" Lynette followed him down the steps and back through the living room where Hayley was giving the baby a bottle and watching a DVD with Tony.

"The study is over here," said Jackson. Lynette followed him into the tastefully decorated study. It definitely had the look of a man cave with its dark leather recliner, big screen TV, and masculine-looking desk.

"Let's box up all these files and desk contents. Grab the laptop too," said Lynette. By this time, another pair of officers had arrived to help with the search. Hours later, Lynette sent the other officers back to the station with the boxes of potential evidence.

"Let's go question our suspects," said Jackson. They went into the living room. Hayley put the baby in the playpen and sent Tony to his room to play. Antonio came in from the kitchen munching on a bagel.

"We found Vicky's purse in your closet. How did it get there?" asked Jackson.

"I've never seen it before," said Antonio

"Me neither," said Hayley. "I cleaned thoroughly the day before the party. I would have noticed that if it had been in my closet."

"Stop playing games. Which one of you took it from Vicky's office the night of the murder? We know you both were there that night," said Lynette.

"So was half the town," shouted Antonio. "Hayley, does your Dad have a good lawyer he can recommend?"

"No need for that yet. You're not under arrest. We're just having a conversation." Jackson hooked his thumbs on his pockets. "You were among the first people who arrived in Vicky's office after she was found dead."

"Well, then someone would have noticed if one of us was holding Vicky's purse," said Hayley. Lynette detected more than a hint of sarcasm in her voice.

"We're just going around in circles. We're going to go through the items we took from the house and we'll get back to you," said Lynette.

Antonio showed them out and slammed he door behind them.

Lynette and Jackson went back to the station and anxiously began going through the laptop and files from Antonio's office. They sent the purse and its contents to the lab. Lynette hoped they'd find fingerprints other than her mom's. "Hey, look at this card," said Lynette. "It's addressed to *boy toy*."

"Well, that means Antonio sent the threatening text we found on Vicky's phone," said Jackson.

"Yes but it was just a threat. Unless we get fingerprints on the purse or some other tangible evidence, we won't have enough to charge him" said Lynette.

"The purse was in his closet. Either he or Hayley had to have put it there. They both knew about the peanut allergy—everyone did. Vicky got the job because of her allergy. Westbrook is a magnet school and they thought Vicky would be the perfect choice since she'd be able to relate."

"My money is on Antonio since he had a stronger motive. I'm sure he didn't want it to be public knowledge that he and Vicky were having an affair," said Lynette.

"But if Hayley found out about the affair she may have been angry enough to kill. She's more likely to have baked cupcakes than Antonio," said Jackson.

"But Antonio had more access. He could have given the cupcake to Vicky any time that day."

"I think we have some more investigating to do," said Jackson.

Chapter 30

Susan was leafing through her new cookbook—*Easy Vegan Meals*. She and Mike were not vegan but she did want to learn some new healthy recipes. *Hmm,* she thought, *this one requires sun-dried tomatoes, nutritional yeast, and something called seitan. Too many weird ingredients.* She flipped to another one. *Hmmm, dice the garlic, chop the bok-choy, and mince the onion. Mince? Too much work. Okay, this one looks good,* she thought as she flipped through a few more pages. Pulse in a food processor…Are you kidding? Any recipe requiring a food processor shouldn't be in a cookbook with the word *easy* in its title. The ring of her cell phone was a welcome interruption.

"Hello."

"Mrs. W, this is Carolina." She was speaking in a quick, high pitched voice.

"What's wrong? Catch your breath and tell me."

"The Department of Children and Families was just here. They wanted to see who was acting as my guardian. Since I'm only sixteen, they said it was against the law for me to be living here alone. I told them the housekeeper stayed here but that wasn't good enough for them. The said they were going to find me a foster family to live with until my dad is able to take care of me." Susan could tell that she was crying.

"Okay, calm down. I'll take you myself if I have to."

"No, they said they had families that were cleared and licensed to take foster children. I said I would get in touch with my grandparents. I don't have any grandparents who are able to do that but I figured it would buy me some time."

"I know a social worker. She works at Westbrook. I'll talk to her about this."

"Thanks, Mrs. W. I don't want to live with strangers."

"Don't worry, that isn't going to happen." As soon as she hung up with Carolina, Susan looked up Jody Decker's number and immediately entered it into her phone.

"Hi, Jody. This is Susan Wiles, we met at the Petrocelli's party on Saturday night."

"Yes, I remember. What can I do for you?"

"Vicky Rogers's daughter, Carolina, just got a visit from the Department of Children and Families. They want to put her in a foster home because she's underage and living on her own. They do have a live-in housekeeper. Her Dad's in rehab trying to get sober. He may be there for several months."

"I'll make some phone calls. They do have grounds to place her in foster care but we can try to delay things. Does she have any other relatives who could take her in?"

"I don't think so. Javier's parents are in Columbia. Vicky's mom is dead and her father is in a nursing home."

"Any aunts, uncles, cousins?" asked Jody.

"I don't think so, but I'll check with Carolina," said Susan.

"I'll make some calls and meanwhile, try to locate a relative. That would be the simplest answer," said Jody.

"Thank you so much. We both appreciate it," replied Susan.

"I'm happy to help," said Jody.

Susan felt a little better. Her head was beginning to hurt so she grabbed some pain killers and a glass of water from the kitchen before calling Carolina back.

"Carolina, I spoke to the social worker I was telling you about. Do you have any relatives who could step in and assume temporary custody while your dad recovers?"

"Not any that I know. Wait, I think my Mom had a sister. She was much younger and I don't think they were close or I would have heard about her. I'll go through her papers again and see if I can find anything."

"Okay. Hang in there. I'll talk to you tomorrow."

Susan hung up and realized that Mike would be back any minute. She hadn't figured out dinner yet and started foraging through the cabinets and fridge. *Well,* she thought. *Pizza it is.* She picked up the phone and called Dominos.

Chapter 31

The smell of garlic and oil permeated the kitchen of the Petrocelli home. Antonio was kneading a mixture of wet chopped meat, egg, and breadcrumbs. Hayley threw the pasta into a big pot of boiling water followed by a dash of salt and a splash of oil. The steam brushed her face. Then she started chopping cucumbers for the salad. The rhythmic sound of the knife against the cutting board was soothing. Hayley had avoided getting into a big discussion over the purse incident with Antonio, just as she'd been avoiding confronting him about his affair with Vicky. He still had no idea that she was aware of his transgressions. "Pass me the tomato," said Hayley.

"Here you go," said Antonio.

"By the way, when do you think we're going to hear more from the police?" asked Hayley.

"I don't know. Probably not until they realize our fingerprints are not on the purse. Then they'll be calling to apologize," said Antonio.

"I still can't fathom how that purse got there. Can you?" Hayley's voice rose at the end as if she expected a confession.

"I have no idea. I didn't put it there so I assumed you did, though I can't imagine why."

"Are you kidding, you idiot? I was sure you did it. I know how upset you were when she didn't recommend you for that vacancy last fall. And I know you had other reasons."

"What other reasons?" said Antonio.

"How stupid do you think I am? Do you think I didn't know you were sleeping with Vicky? What...did you hope it would get you ahead in your career or were you just turned off by your wife—the wife who'd just given birth and was still carrying around a few extra pounds."

"No, Hayley, I would never have done that to you." Hayley couldn't believe how phony he sounded.

"Don't even pretend. I have proof and you'll pay for treating me that way," said Hayley.

"So that's what this is about. You took the purse to frame me. You killed Vicky with one of your cupcakes and then planted the purse in the closet so I'd be blamed."

"Oh, yeah, that's right. Me. A cold-blooded killer. If 'I'd killed her, I certainly wouldn't have put the purse in my own house. I would have disposed of it ASAP or just left it there."

"Why didn't you listen to your parents and marry someone rich in the first place? You never thought I was good enough for you. You figured you'd get me thrown in jail for murder so you'd get rid of me."

"Wow, I can't believe your acting career never took off." Just then Tony called form the living room.

"Mommy, I'm hungry. When's dinner?"

"In just a little while, honey." She whispered to Antonio, "I don't want him to hear us fighting. Let's shelve this for now."

"For now," said Antonio. He threw the meatballs in the pan, into the hot oil.

Chapter 32

The winding dirt road seemed much less ominous in the daylight. *At least I know where this ends*, thought Susan. She'd picked up Carolina early from school so they could visit Javier and try to get closer to finding a relative.

"Thanks for doing this Mrs. W," said Carolina. "I can't wait to see him."

"I'm as anxious as you are to get this settled. There's no way you're going to go to a foster home." The ride seemed much shorter than when she'd come here with Lynette. Before she knew it, Susan saw the Rehab sign and pulled into the parking lot.

"Do I look okay?" asked Carolina. She applied a little cherry lip gloss

"You look beautiful, as always," said Susan.

Carolina had her hair pulled back into a low ponytail. *I couldn't have gotten my big toe into those skinny jeans even when I was sixteen*, thought Susan, but she admired how even though they were form-fitting, they looked tasteful. Some teenage girls wore those jeans that were all ripped and shredded looking. They walked into the lobby. Although the rehab could almost pass for a hotel, the hospital smell gave it away. Susan pressed the elevator button and they waited as the orange numbers blinked and the metal door opened. They found Javier's room and Carolina embraced her dad with a hearty bear hug.

"You look beautiful, *mi hija*. I've missed you so much," said Javier.

"I've missed you too. I'm so proud of you, taking this step."

"I'm doing it for you. When I finish here we will put our family life back together. I know it won't be the same without your mom but we will be okay."

"I know." Carolina's face relaxed and she smiled. It was the first time since before Vicky's death that Susan had seen that smile.

"Does either one of you know what's happening with the murder investigation? I may have had my share of problems with Vicky, but I want to know who did this to her. The killer took away my baby's mother. He deserves to be locked up in jail for the rest of his life," said Javier.

"I know," said Carolina. I won't be able to even start dealing with this until the murderer is found. I want to know why he killed my Mom," said Carolina.

"The Westbrook Police Department is working hard on this case. My daughter Lynette is a detective on the force and I know she'll solve this. She's brilliant," said Susan. She remembered the primary reason they'd come here and subtly changed the subject.

"Javier, we need to find a relative to stay with Carolina until you get out or she'll be placed with a foster family."

"Foster family?" Javier rose from the edge of the bed. "No way. Isn't Araceli still living at the house?"

"Yes, but they won't accept her as a guardian," answered Susan.

"Then I'm checking myself out right now. I'm coming home with you." Javier opened the drawer and grabbed his underwear and a pair of jeans.

"No, Dad. You need to get yourself together.' Carolina grabbed the jeans and put them back in the drawer. "I was thinking, didn't mom once say she had a sister?" asked Carolina.

"Oh, yes, but they hadn't spoken to each other in years," said Javier.

"Do you know how I can get in touch with her?" asked Carolina.

"I have no idea, none at all. I don't even remember her name. I think it started with an R. Maybe it was Regina or something. The best thing to do would be to call Grandpa in Florida. It's his daughter after all," said Javier.

"Yes, but according to mom he was in pretty bad shape," said Carolina.

"He's in and out. It's worth a try. I think I even have the number of the nursing home here in my phone. I called to tell him that Vicky had died but I'm not sure he understood." He scrolled through his phone and gave Carolina the number.

"Let's try him right now," said Carolina. She entered the number and pressed the call button.

"Coventry Assisted Living and Nursing Home. How may I direct your call?" asked the operator.

Carolina explained that she wanted to speak to her grandfather and was connected to his room.

"Hello, Grandpa? This is Carolina. What? I can't understand you. What are you saying? Grandpa, I need your help. Grandpa?" Carolina paused and then began speaking again. "Yes, thank you, ma'am. Okay. I understand." Carolina ended the call and turned to Susan and her father.

"Well, I guess we're back at square one," said Carolina. "The voice that answered was incoherent. A nurse took the phone and explained that my Grandfather is in an advanced stage of dementia. Although he still has moments when he seems perfectly normal, these, according to the nurse, are getting less frequent."

"I think you need to fly down there," said Susan.

"Maybe if you see him in person he'll be able to focus," said Javier.

"That's a great idea," said Carolina.

"The flight is only a few hours and I'll even go with you," said Susan.

"Really? That would be great. Thank you, Mrs. W."

"Yes, thank you," said Javier. "I feel so much better knowing you are watching out for my daughter." Javier gave Carolina a big hug and a kiss on the cheek.

Susan and Carolina headed back home. While Susan drove, Carolina called the airline and booked a flight for the next morning.

Chapter 33

Jody sat down at the Starbuck's counter and waited for Theresa. The robust coffee smell wafted through the entire store. She preferred a latte to a beer any day. The store itself was buzzing like a triple espresso grande. *I already feel more awake and I haven't even ordered yet,* thought Jody. *How is it that this place is always booming, even late in the afternoon?* She scanned the shop looking for Theresa. *Look at that father buying his son a coffee. That kid is maybe ten. As a matter of fact, I think he goes to our school. I hate when parents are so clueless. Doesn't he know kids shouldn't be drinking coffee? Caffeine is a drug. He might as well be giving the kid cocaine.*

"Hey, sorry I'm late." Theresa came in still wearing her work clothes. "Let's get in line. I really need some coffee. Maybe a biscotti too. We can hit the gym tomorrow."

"I just got here. How are things going? Tell me about that new guy you're seeing. You've been walking on a cloud these days."

"Well, he's just wonderful. He buys me flowers and texts me all the time saying he's thinking about me. We've been together every day this week. I think he may be *the one*." Theresa looked like a star-gazing teenager.

"I'm very happy for you. He just better keep treating you right or he'll have me to answer to. What are friends for, right?"

"I'm glad you've got my back," giggled Theresa. "Hey, we're next."

"I'll take a mocha latte with soy milk and a chocolate biscotti," said Theresa.

"I'll take a frappacino with whipped cream. It's been a tough day," Jody said. They found an empty table and enjoyed their drinks.

Chapter 34

I hate traveling these days, thought Susan. *It's such a hassle taking off your shoes, packing three ounces of shampoo, taking your laptop out of the case.* As a rule, she avoided air travel but this was important. She hoped Carolina would get the information she needed.

Carolina looked at the flight board. "Hey, it looks like the flight's on time," said Carolina.

Susan was glad the weather had cooperated. She and Carolina took out their self-printed boarding passes. Neither had luggage to check, which would save time when they got to Ft. Lauderdale. They boarded the plane.

"I wish they had more storage for carry-ons," said Susan. She checked a few overhead bins and finally found room to store her suitcase. Carolina shoved her soft duffel bag under her seat. Susan took out her Kindle. Carolina took out her iPod. The flight was smooth and before they knew it, they were in Florida.

"I hope we get some answers," said Carolina. "I don't want to worry about being taken away from my home. I've lost so much already."

"I know," said Susan. She took off her jacket but noticed that there were people wearing jeans and sweaters. "I definitely consider this shorts weather," she said. The air was thick and heavy even though this was technically winter. She'd been to Florida in the summer and it was even stickier and hotter. She didn't understand why people retired here. She loved the change of seasons in New York and really hated the heat. At least summer only lasted a few months back home.

"Here's the hotel shuttle," said Carolina. They climbed into the white van and buckled up. "The roads are so flat here," said Carolina. Back in the Hudson Valley they were surrounded by mountains so this was a noticeable contrast. They pulled into the Ramada Inn, gathered their bags, and checked in.

The room was generic .There were two full-sized beds with floral bedspreads, a dark wood desk, and a bathroom with a tub/shower combo. *It's so stuffy in here,* thought Susan. She turned the air conditioner to high while Carolina flicked on some lamps and opened the curtains. They put their clothes in the dresser drawers. Susan put her toothbrush and three ounces of shampoo in the bathroom.

"Let's grab a quick lunch and then get over to the nursing home," suggested Susan.

"Sure. Let me just change my clothes first. I'm sweaty from the van ride. You think they'd use the AC." Carolina put on a fresh pair of jeans and a T shirt which read 'Westbury High Debate Team.'

"Is this okay?" asked Susan. They were standing in front of the hotel café.

"Sure. I'm anxious to eat and get going," said Carolina.

"They have a lunch special. You can get either soup or a salad with half a Cuban sandwich," explained Susan.

"I'll get that with the minestrone," said Carolina.

"I'll have the same," said Susan.

They ate their overpriced soup and sandwiches, and then grabbed a black and yellow taxi from the line in front of the hotel.

"Look at those houses," said Carolina. The taxi was driving along the ocean on A1A. The mansions were mostly Spanish-styled with iron sculpted gates and fountains out front. The taxi driver explained that most of the owners only came down for the winters.

Coventry was a newer building with a salmon-colored exterior. The lobby was painted pastel blue and a large mural with palm trees flanking a beach scene was the first thing you saw when you walked in. Wicker furniture was arranged so that it was possible for ambulatory residents to come out and visit with their families. Susan and Carolina were buzzed into the facility. The first thing that hit them was the smell of body odor. Susan had seen an experiment on Dr. Oz where they took t-shirts and had three different aged groups of people wear them for a week. Then they had audience members smell them and rate the odor. The shirts from the oldest wearers were rated least offensive. Susan didn't buy that. There definitely was such a thing as old person smell and it wasn't pleasant. She gave her armpit a discreet sniff, just in case. They passed patients in wheelchairs and others with walkers. The halls had railings built into both sides of the walls. It was depressing, no way around it.

"Here's his room," said Carolina. The room was small and painted yellow with a green and white patterned wall paper border. In the center was a utilitarian hospital bed with a metal night stand. Across from the bed, a flat screen TV was suspended from the ceiling. A faux wood dresser and a plastic chair rounded out the décor. They walked in and saw an elderly man lying on his side in a fetal position. Susan was less than optimistic that they'd be able to communicate with him. She was right.

"Mr. Bowers, my name is Susan Wiles and this is Carolina Rogers, your granddaughter. We came from New York to see you."

Mr. Bowers grunted.

"Grandpa, do you remember me?" asked Carolina. She turned to Susan. "I haven't seen him since I was eight. I'll be surprised if he recognizes me."

"Mr. Bowers, we really need to talk to you. Carolina needs your help."

Mr. Bowers was unresponsive. A nurse came in to check his blood pressure.

"He has his good days and his bad," said the nurse. "If you catch him at the right time, he's perfectly lucid. Maybe come back later,"

"Thank you," said Carolina. "I guess we have no choice."

"Don't worry. We'll try again later. The nurse said he goes in and out."

Susan and Carolina returned to the hotel.

"I brought a bathing suit just in case," said Susan. "Why don't we go down to the pool for a bit? We can try again after dinner."

"Okay, I guess so," said Carolina. Carolina pulled a striped two-piece from her suitcase. Susan changed into a black one-piece. She hated black but she knew it made you look slimmer—especially when combined with 'tummy trimming technology.' They grabbed-shaped pool.

"The water is so refreshing," said Susan. Surprisingly, they had the whole pool to themselves. The pool was lined with white plastic lounge chairs and in the corner there was a table covered with an umbrella. If it weren't for the sound of the traffic whizzing by, you could almost think you were in some Caribbean resort. Well....maybe a Caribbean Econolodge.

"It feels so weird to be swimming outdoors in the middle of winter," said Carolina. "I could get used to this. Strange as it may seem, I love the smell of chlorine."

Susan did a little aqua jogging. It was easier on your joints than jogging on land and the water added resistance. After a while, a family with two children came through the gate. The little boy looked like a third grader, and the little girl—kindergarten. After spending her career teaching in an elementary school, Susan could easily assess a child's age.

"Hello," said the dad. He was probably in his mid-thirties and wore light blue surfer shorts. "Where are you girls from?"

"New York," answered Susan. "And you?"

"Atlanta. We're here for my father's birthday. He loves seeing the kids."

"I'm sure he does," answered Susan. She knew she'd love spending time with her grandchildren one day. The mom was about the same age as the dad and wore a modest two piece. She swam a few laps, then stretched her arms over the side of the pool, kicking her feet nonchalantly out in front of her. The children were both experienced swimmers and raced back and forth across the pool. When they got tired of that, the little boy started jumping off the side of the pool and deliberately splashing his sister.

"Mom, tell him to stop," whined the little girl, stretching the word *Mom* into two syllables. That's something Susan didn't miss from her teaching days. She hated when kids used that whiney tone. Lynette would never let her kids get away with that. No, siree, her grandkids would know how to use their words to effectively communicate. No need for dramatics.

"Well, I think we're going to dry off and get some dinner. It was nice meeting you. Have fun with your Grandpa." Susan addressed the last comment to the children.

When they got back to the room, Susan called Mike. She already missed him. She and Carolina changed out of their bathing suits and put on fresh clothes for dinner.

"I'm going to hang my suit here by the air conditioner," said Carolina.

"What do you feel like eating?" asked Susan.

"I saw a pizza place," said Carolina. "We passed it on the way to the nursing home. Let's eat there and then go back to see my Grandfather."

"Sounds good," said Susan.

They entered the pizzeria and took a seat at a booth. The table was covered with a red and white checkered tablecloth, and a wax-covered Chianti bottle had been turned into a table light. Susan and Carolina studied the plastic menus.

"Let's share a pizza if that's okay with you," said Susan. "What do you want on it? Do you want New York style or Sicilian?"

"New York style has fewer calories, and I like mushrooms and black olives."

"Sounds perfect. Let's get the whole wheat crust."

After dinner, they returned to the nursing home. Mr. Bowers was sitting up, eating his dinner with the help of the nurse. Compared to the delicious pizza they'd just eaten, his dinner looked horrid.

"Hi, Grandpa. Are you enjoying your dinner?" Mr. Bowers looked at Carolina and said something that sounded like gibberish. He was eating mashed potatoes and some meatloaf that looked as though it had been left out in the rain. The hospital sheets were tossed aside. Susan was grateful that he was wearing pajama pants under his hospital gown.

"How is he this evening?" asked Susan

"He was talking a bit before dinner, then he lapsed back into this," said the nurse.

"Carolina," said Mr. Bowers.

"I'm surprised that he knows my name and can say it so clearly." His knees were bent like a door jamb in need of oil. Protruding from his hospital gown, his legs looked like deflated footballs.

"Grandpa, yes it's me." Carolina moved closer and grasped his forearm.

"Carolina. Remember the rocking horse?"

"Yes, Grandpa." Carolina looked at Susan. "I think he remembers how I used to love the rocking horse outside Safeway. It was painted black and white with red stirrups and black plastic reins. He had to give me a boost to reach the saddle. He used to put quarter after quarter in the red metal box for me. It even played cowboy music. Grandpa would sing along, something about 'git along little dogies'."

"Carolina," aid Mr. Bowers.

"I don't think you'll get much more right now. Why don't you give me your phone number and I'll call you if he becomes coherent," offered the nurse.

"Okay, let's do that," said Carolina. Carolina jotted down her number on the pad of paper on the nightstand. Susan could hear the disappointment in Carolina's voice. They found a taxi and returned to the hotel. Carolina pulled out her smart phone, and Susan turned on the TV.

"We'll try again tomorrow," said Susan. "I know you're disappointed but tomorrow is, as they say, another day. Let's relax and get some sleep."

"Okay. I think I'll take a shower now so I'll have time to dry my hair."

Susan set her phone alarm and watched a little more TV before falling asleep. How did *Law and Order* manage to stay so interesting after all these years? You'd think they'd run out of ideas for episodes. She could hear the cars going by outside but she was used to Mike's snoring so she had no problem falling asleep.

No Ambien needed. The ringing of Carolina's cell phone woke her up before sunrise. She could hear Carolina groggily answer the phone.

"Hello. Yes, this is Mr. Bower's granddaughter. Really? Thank you so much. We'll be right over."

"Well, was it the nursing home?" asked Susan. By now she was fully awake and craving coffee.

"Yes, it was the nurse from last night. Her shift ends at 7:00 so she wanted to call us before she left to tell us that Grandpa is awake and is totally coherent. She knew we'd be anxious to come over."

"Oh, that's great. Let me jump in the shower and we'll get over there. I'll be very fast." Susan was true to her word. Five minutes later she pulled a pair of tan capris and a coral colored t-shirt from the drawer. Wearing summer clothes in the middle of winter felt weird but it was refreshing not to be restricted by bulky clothing. Outside of the lobby, the sunrise painted pastels across the horizon and the wind blew a hint of coolness across her cheek. Pedestrians carried coffee and newspapers. Why did coffee always smell especially enticing on mornings when you most needed it? Susan felt a slight ache across her forehead. Joggers and bikers competed for space on the sidewalk. *Don't people go to work here in Florida*, thought Susan. Certainly not all of the morning exercisers looked old enough to be retired. A line of yellow taxis were parked outside of the hotel. Susan and Carolina slid into the first one and despite morning traffic, they walked through the nursing home doors twenty minutes later.

"I hope he's still talking," said Carolina. She clasped her hands together as though she was praying.

"Well, let's find out," said Susan. They signed in at the front desk and stuck blue and white visitor passes to their shirts. The aroma of bacon and eggs emanated from the food carts that lined the hallways. Susan's stomach growled. When they got to Mr. Bower's room they were astonished to see Carolina's grandpa sitting up in bed. His hair was combed and he looked twenty years younger than he'd looked yesterday.

"Hi, Grandpa," said Carolina. She went over to the bed and gave him a hug.

"Carolina. I'd recognize that beautiful face anywhere. You look so grown up. I'm so happy to see you." He hugged her with his scrawny arms.

"You too, Grandpa. This is my friend Mrs. Wiles. She was the best teacher ever and she's been watching out for me ever since mom died."

"Good, good. How is your Dad doing?"

"He's doing just great," said Carolina. Susan knew the whole subject of Javier drinking and having been a suspect in Vicky's murder was not something Carolina wanted to get into.

"What can I do for you, sweetheart?" His cloudy blue eyes looked up at Carolina.

"I'm hoping you can help me find my mom's sister––your younger daughter."

"Oh, yes, Rebecca."

"Does she live around here?" asked Carolina.

"No, she lives in Idaho—no, wait, Ohio. She works at some daycare or school or maybe a college. She comes down here sometimes. I saw her yesterday. She brought cookies."

"That was last summer, Mr. Bowers. Remember, she came for your birthday," interrupted the nurse.

"Do you know why mom never talked about her?" asked Carolina.

"Yes, it was so sad. They haven't talked since Rosemary's death. Your Grandma Rosemary died when you were a little girl last year. I wish you could have known her. She was a great cook—made the best meatloaf, even used fresh tomatoes in it. I used to tell her it was what got me to propose to her."

Carolina seemed to be getting a little impatient. "What happened?"

"Trouble. Trouble over the inheritance. Rosemary left the gems to Rebecca, gave Vicky nothing. I guess she figured since Vicky was married and already set with a good career she didn't need it. Boy, your mom had a temper. Used to throw things and slam doors when she got mad. I don't really blame her for being upset, but it wasn't Rebecca who wrote the will. Rebecca probably would have shared some of it with her had she not overreacted so badly."

"Wow. I had no idea. I think mom mentioned having a sister maybe once. I have an aunt that I've never even met. Is she married? Does she have kids?"

"No, not yet .She's so pretty, like her mom," said Mr. Bowers.

"Carolina, we passed a bagel shop on our way here. It was only about a block away. You visit and I'll bring back some breakfast." Susan walked past more joggers and bicyclists en route to the bagel shop. She imagined those joggers stopping there to carb load. Bins of bagels and bialys greeted customers as soon as they walked in the door. So many choices, she thought—onion, sesame, poppy seed, raisin. She chose the whole wheat one for herself and an assortment to bring back to the nursing home. The shop was crowded with diners and the take-out line was growing by the minute. Waitresses zipped through refilling coffee and delivering red plastic baskets of food. The bagels were still warm when she received her order. She could feel the heat through the brown paper bag and the yeasty, doughy aroma taunted her all the way back to Coventry. She figured it was about half a mile each way. The promise of bagels (and coffee) had her power walking all the way back. She figured this walk could maybe burn up about the calories in the butter she was going to put on her bagel.

Carolina and her Grandpa were still talking when she returned. Susan offered a bagel to the nurse.

"This salt bagel tastes just like a pretzel," said Carolina.

"I'm afraid I can only handle the soft part in the middle. My teeth aren't what they used to be," said Grandpa.

They finished breakfast together before saying their goodbyes. *Dementia was a strange animal*, thought Susan. She hoped that she and Mike would be spared that experience as they continued to age. Susan was thankful that Carolina had gotten to spend time with her grandfather and that she'd found out about her aunt. She and Carolina went back to the hotel, packed, and boarded a plane for home.

Chapter 35

Theresa wiggled into a low cut black cocktail dress with spaghetti straps. She'd carefully chosen this to wear on this special evening. After a long hiatus, Theresa was finally dating again. As a matter of fact, that detective Jackson Simpson had even tried to ask her out. When it rains it pours. He was kind of dorky but had she not already met David, she might have given him a shot. She slipped on a pair of heels that she'd worn maybe once in the past five years. They were stiletto heels, highly out of character for her, but she did appreciate the extra height. Jody had talked her into wearing them for her big date. Jody loved heels— she insisted they made your legs look sexy. Theresa put on her makeup in the bathroom mirror, following the steps for creating 'dramatic cat eyes' that she'd seen in *Cosmo*. Afterwards, she spun around and checked herself out in the bedroom mirror. *There*, she thought. *Not bad at all if I say so myself.* When the doorbell rang, she grabbed her beaded purse and opened the door.

"You look stunning," said David. The clean shaven man standing in the doorway towered over Theresa by nearly a foot. His shoulders were broad and had he not been dressed in an expensive suit and silk tie, Theresa swore he could be mistaken for one of the Jet's running backs. Well, maybe a retired running back. He was older than Theresa by about a decade.

David exhibited manners and maturity. He owned his own business and was financially stable, unlike many of the other men she'd dated. Theresa was an old-fashioned girl at heart and appreciated when a guy held doors open and treated you to dinner. David's vending machine business was the reason they met. One day he came to school to install a new vending machine in the teacher's lounge (one that didn't sell peanuts). He installed it himself, showing his muscles as he wheeled it into the school and lifted it off the dolly. She wasn't the only one who noticed his buff biceps. The lounge buzzed about how he belonged in the *Hot Firefighter's Calendar* or how maybe he danced for Chippendale's on the side. He came back weekly to check on the machine and they started talking. Then he asked her out and she hadn't stopped smiling since. Tonight he was taking her into the city for dinner and a Broadway show.

"Let's go, Beautiful," said David. He walked her out to his silver BMW and opened the door for her. She was expecting the back of her thighs to freeze when she sat down but was pleasantly surprised. She'd never been in a car with a seat warmer before—this was luxury at its best.

"So, where are we eating?" she asked.

"A trendy new steak house near the theater. You're going to love it."

Theresa didn't eat red meat as a rule but she'd make an exception. When they arrived, David valet-parked the BMW and led her in by the arm. *What a gentleman*, she thought. The steward brought the wine list and without hesitation, David ordered an expensive bottle of red wine.

"You're going to love this," said David. David refused the menus and ordered fillet mignon for both of them.

"We'll have them medium rare, with rice pilaf on the side and let's start with some French onion soup," he told the waiter. Theresa hated onions and preferred her steak well done when she ate it at all, but said nothing. David had a take charge manner about him that didn't invite negotiation.

"This looks delicious," said Theresa, when the food finally arrived. David had very good taste. She cut and sampled a piece of the filet.

"I knew you'd like it," said David.

The restaurant dripped with elegance. Classical music played softly and vanilla-scented candles glowed on each of the round tables, making David appear even dreamier than he was. The waiters wore tuxedos and white gloves. After dinner, they strolled down the bustling street which was alive with the lights and sounds of the city. Bright marquees advertised a plethora of plays. A violinist played again, his hat on the ground inviting donations. Cars honked in the distance. Fur clad women on the arms of silver-haired escorts, younger couples in jeans, groups of girlfriends in micro minis, tourists dressed in their Sunday best— all on their way to see the world's finest selection of theater.

They walked through the doors of the Schubert Theater and sank into plush, red velvet, orchestra level seats. If she had to describe the theater in one word, Theresa would have chosen *gold.* The walls dripped gold. Although she'd never been to France, Theresa had seen pictures of Versailles and this theater reminded her of it. The house lights dimmed and Theresa recognized one of the actresses from a soap opera she used to watch with her grandmother. During intermission, they meandered into the lobby and enjoyed a glass of wine. Theresa loved theater and was sorry when the actors came out for the final curtain call.

"The show was fantastic," said Theresa, as David escorted her back to the valet stand. She didn't want the night to end.

"As was the company," added David. "Our chariot awaits."

The silver BMW was Theresa's horse drawn carriage and the stilettos were her glass slippers. Theresa was falling in love with Prince Charming.

Chapter 36

It was quieter than normal when Lynette and Jackson came back in from lunch. Lynette smelled onions as soon as they walked into the station. Lynette guessed that Officer Collins had been eating an Italian hoagie. In the back corner of the station, Detective Valentino was talking to a young mother and her son. As they got closer, Lynette overheard the mother reporting a stolen bike. Lynette and Jackson were still consumed with Vicky's murder.

"I wish we could link Hayley or Antonio to the murder but the purse alone isn't enough," said Lynette.

"We know that Antonio is *boy toy* but that isn't proof of murder either. It's all circumstantial," said Jackson. He rubbed his chin.

"I've been searching records," said Lynette. "I've uncovered another piece of possible evidence. It's a bit of a stretch but may be worth looking into." She turned the computer screen so Jackson could see it too.

"This is a lawsuit that Vicky filed against Rebecca Bowers. She's suing for full claim to her mother's estate. This has to be her sister," said Lynette. "I have an address and phone number for her in Columbus, Ohio, but I can't reach her."

"Call the Columbus Police Department," suggested Jackson.

"I already sent them an email. Hopefully they'll follow up soon."

"You know something," said Jackson. "It bothers me that we didn't find the Epi-pen that Vicky supposedly had in her office desk drawer. There was one in the purse, which explains why either Antonio or Hayley might have taken it, but wouldn't they have thrown the second one in the purse too?"

"I know," said Lynette. "It's perplexing." Just then the phone on Lynette's desk rang. It was the Columbus Police Department.

"We got your email and followed up on the address you gave us. Rebecca Bowers no longer lives there. The landlord said she moved out a few months ago and he doesn't have a forwarding address. The university says she works online from home. They have the old address too."

"I'll contact her through her university email," said Lynette. "Hopefully, she'll respond. Thank you for getting back to me so quickly."

"Anytime we can help, just let us know," said the officer.

Lynette searched for Rebecca's university email address and wrote, requesting that she contact her. Meanwhile, she continued her records search.

"Look, Jackson. It's a countersuit filed by Rebecca Bowers against Vicky. If Vicky was threatening to take the entire estate, maybe Rebecca had a motive for murder."

Chapter 37

"Want to grab a drink after work?" asked Jody. Theresa had come into the office for lunch. Jody was happy to take a break. She'd spent the morning working on a case involving a second grader who was being teased because she dressed in boy's clothing every day and played soccer with the boys at recess. Some of the kids in the class had been calling her 'gay.' Can you imagine? Second graders already knew how hurtful those words could be. She called the parents in for a conference. Instead of being furious about the kids calling their child gay, they actually were mad at their daughter for dressing like a boy. Jody clenched her fists.

"Sure, as long as I'm back by 6:00. David is taking me out to dinner and he'll be upset if I am late."

"So things are still going great?"

"Sure." Theresa gazed down at the floor. The phone on Jody's desk rang.

"Hello, this is Ms. Decker."

"Hello, Jody, this is Susan Wiles."

"Hi, Susan. What can I do for you?"

"Carolina and I just got back from Florida. We saw Carolina's grandfather and found out that Vicky did have a younger sister named Rebecca. We found out that she lives in Ohio (or possibly Idaho) and have been trying to find her. I'm confident that we'll be able to find her. Anyhow, since Carolina does have an aunt, can you let the Department of Children and Families know that we're in the process of working out custody with her aunt?"

"Yes, I'll fudge it a bit and say you've already spoken to her. That will buy us some time but you'll need to find her soon."

"I know. Maybe I'll see if Lynette can help. I really appreciate this Jody."

"Glad I could help. Keep me posted." Jody hung up the phone.

"So, I see Mr. Petrocelli has moved into Vicky's office," said Theresa.

"Yes, the minute they removed the police tape, he wa—'Antonio Petrocelli, *Principal.*' He must have paid extra for next day shipping."

"Have you heard anything else about the murder?"

"Hayley was here a few days ago. I wasn't eavesdropping, but since my office is right next door, I heard her arguing with Antonio. She was accusing him of taking Vicky's purse the night of the murder. Apparently, they found it in a closet at his house."

"Wow, that's so weird. Do you think he took it?" asked Theresa.

"Who knows? He's been living high on the hog since she died. He insisted he didn't take it…he even accused Hayley of taking it. That made no sense to me." Jody sat back in her chair and folded her arms.

"Well, there you are." David stormed into Jody's office and addressed Theresa. His denim shirt was half tucked into his jeans and his hair was mussed. "Why weren't you eating in the teacher's lounge? I was looking all over for you."

"I didn't expect to see you here. We're supposed to meet tonight for dinner," said Theresa.

"I had to check on the vending machine so I thought I'd check on you too." David finally acknowledged Jody.

"So you're my competition for Theresa's attention." Jody noticed the corners of David's mouth curl into a smirk.

"We're good friends. I stay out of the way of her love life," said Jody.

"I'll see you after work, Jody," said Theresa. "Come on David. I'll walk you out. I need to pick up my class." Theresa and David left and several minutes later Sandra came into Jody's office with a phone message.

"So, what was Macho Man doing here?" ask Sandra. "I haven't seen him in here since Vicky died.

"Macho Man?" asked Jody

"He comes in wearing a t-shirt in the middle of winter just to show off his muscles. One day he came in here carrying a huge box of replacement snacks for the vending machine. We told him we had a cart, but he insisted he could carry it himself so we nicknamed him Macho Man. I think Vicky was the one who came up with that," said Sandy.

Chapter 38

Oatmeal again, thought Susan. Those gross-looking green shakes that she saw on Dr. Oz might not be such a bad alternative after all. Susan had two things on her mind—finding Rebecca Bowers, and linking Antonio to Vicky's murder. She tried calling the number she got from the nurse at Coventry, but a recording revealed that Rebecca's phone had been disconnected. Next, she opened her laptop. She tried searching for Rebecca on Facebook but to no avail. She never could understand the obsession some of her friends had with Facebook, but when she realized she'd be able to post pictures of her grandchild—when she had a grandchild—it all made sense.

She filled the cat bowls with Meow Mix and poured herself a second cup of coffee. She opened the curtains so that she and the cats could enjoy the morning sunlight. Then she realized she hadn't yet shared the information about Rebecca with Lynette. *I think I'll take a ride down to the station,* she thought. She grabbed her down jacket and pulled on her fur-lined boots. There was a light dusting of snow on the ground and flurries were falling. It didn't take long to get to the station. She walked in and was greeted by her favorite keystone cop.

"Well, if it isn't Miss Marple," said Jackson. He stood with his hands on his hips. *He's trying to look taller*, thought Susan. She thought he kind of resembled a penguin. Susan wasn't at all surprised that he wasn't married.

"Well, hello, Barney Fife. Where's Lynette?" asked Susan.

"Here to help us solve the case? Did you get back any DNA evidence? Talk to the local psychic?" chided Jackson.

"Why, yes. The local medium told me to beware of a short, squatty know-it-all cop who needed all the assistance he could get. She said I'd better hurry," said Susan.

Just then, Lynette came out of her office. *She looks exhausted*, thought Susan. *It's no wonder. It must be awful getting daily hormone shots and going to the lab for blood work before work.*

"Hi, Mom, what's going on?" said Lynette.

"I wanted to tell you about the trip Carolina and I took to Florida." Susan took a seat. "We saw Carolina's grandfather at the nursing home. He told us that Vicky has a younger sister. Her name is Rebecca and there were problems between the sisters. Rebecca inherited her mother's entire gem collection upon her death. Their mother Rosemary left nothing to Vicky so Vicky was suing her for the estate. She lives in Ohio. I have a phone number but it's been disconnected."

"Good job, Turbo," said Jackson. "We had that information already."

"Thanks, Mom. We've been looking into it. We found out that Rebecca is employed by Ohio State but she works from home. She moved out of her apartment and no one knows where she is now. I sent her an email but so far no response."

"I'm trying to find her in hopes she will act as Carolina's guardian while Javier is in rehab," said Susan.

"We're trying to find her because she had a motive for killing Vicky. That gem collection was worth just under a million dollars," said Susan.

Chapter 39

Carolina got out of the old yellow school bus and walked up the circular driveway carrying a backpack stuffed full of text books. She tightened her red wool scarf around her neck and took the mittens out of her pockets. *They should just give us all iPads*, she thought. Some schools were doing that. Then she wouldn't be risking a lumbar strain from lugging around ten pounds of books. She used to text her Mom every day on the way from the bus to the door to let her know she was home. Mom had still been at work but she always had a 'to-do' list for her. It usually involved throwing a load of wash in or unloading the dishwasher—and more often than not, starting dinner. She used to get annoyed—what was the point in having a housekeeper then? But her mom pointed out that Araceli had plenty to do and Carolina needed to learn how to do these things since she'd be going to college in the blink of an eye. Carolina put on her invisible headphones and tuned her out whenever that lecture started.

Powdery snow had fallen last night and blanketed the driveway. Carolina wondered what she'd do if there was a blizzard and Dad wasn't here to shovel. Then she remembered that she didn't drive anyway so it didn't matter. That was another thing. Her dad was supposed to be teaching her how to drive. Mom was supposed to help her choose a prom dress this spring—if she had a date. She thought about that quote she heard in Language Arts—"...the best laid plans of mice and men oft times go astray." Boy had they ever.

That's strange, thought Carolina. She noticed tread marks in the snow. No one should have come to the house while she was at school. Araceli lived there but her car was parked inside the garage and there weren't any tire marks in front of the garage door. She looked for a package at the door thinking maybe it was the UPS man but the front stoop was empty. She stomped the snow off her feet and turned the key in the front door. Araceli was vacuuming the living room. She was startled when Carolina came up behind her and said hello. "Hi, sweetie, how was school?"

"It was fine. Did anyone come by today? I saw tire tracks in the driveway."

"No, nobody came." Araceli smoothed her apron. "I started some *ropa vieja*. I thought you'd appreciate a real meal since you've been living on Lean Cuisines."

"Thanks, it smells wonderful." Carolina opened the fridge. She grabbed a package of baby carrots with ranch dressing and a Diet Coke. Then she lugged her backpack into her room and started her homework. She was taking three advanced placement courses and there was a lot of homework. She was proud of herself for keeping up her grades throughout this turmoil. In some ways, studying offered a much needed escape for the anger and sadness she dealt with on a daily basis.

Chapter 40

When she'd used Google Earth to pinpoint the town, Rebecca Bowers wasn't sure what she'd be getting into. All she knew was that she had to move there. She had to keep an eye on things. She enjoyed living in the city and being part of the university so it was with reticence that she left her life behind for Westbrook. She packed up her Ford Focus and headed east towards New York. Thank God, she'd gotten the air conditioning in her car fixed last month. The northeast was having a heat wave. The closer she got to New York the more oppressive the air felt. She was pleasantly surprised when she arrived in Westbrook, in the sticky dog days of summer. Everywhere she looked it was green. Trees were laden with leaves, and dandelions punctuated the golf course-like green lawns. You could smell the humidity in the air all day long until late afternoon thunderstorms passed. What a charming little town this was—close to the big city…yet so far away.

Rebecca was getting ready to meet her gym friends for dinner. She pulled her wavy brown hair into a high ponytail. She'd gotten it cut right before the move. It had been very long—all the way to where her butt started. In her three decades of life, she remembered getting it trimmed maybe half a dozen times. At least Locks of Love will be able to make a few wigs out of this donation, she remembered thinking at the time. It somewhat eased the pain of giving up her youthful persona for a mature one. It was time to step up to the plate and take charge of things.

Chapter 41

Vinnie's Pizzeria was always busy. It was a Wednesday night and Jody and Theresa actually had to wait for a table as if it were a Saturday night. The chef was putting a pizza into the brick oven using a wooden board with an extra long handle. While they waited to be seated, people continually came up to the counter, picking up white boxes to carry home for dinner. Theresa wore jeans and a button-down shirt under her jacket. Jody wore corduroys and boots, projecting a retro look. She wasn't crazy about the clunky boots but it was hard to find delicate ones in her size.

"Right this way." The hostess led them to a table and gave them menus.

"We'll need a third place setting," said Jody. Then they ordered a pitcher of beer.

"So how are things going with David?" asked Jody.

"Okay. He's a bit possessive though. An old friend who happens to be a guy came to visit last week. David really gave me the third degree and insisted on coming along for dinner. He gets jealous if I even mention a man's name."

"Hey, sorry I'm late." Rebecca took off her coat and sat down.

"No problem, Becky. Have some beer. How are things going?" asked Jody.

"Everything's good. My legs are still sore from the kickboxing we did yesterday. It's midterms time so I've had a lot of grading to keep up with," said Becky.

"At least you get to work in your pajamas," said Theresa

"Well, it's not always easy. There are too many temptations like sleeping in and watching *The View*. It's nice to get out and spend some time with friends. It gives me a reason to get dressed."

As she smiled, Jody couldn't help noticing that Becky's teeth were as straight as the guards outside of Buckingham Palace. And they were so white. Either she completely shunned wine, coffee, and any other potentially staining foods, or she'd recently engaged in tooth whitening.

A waitress who was dressed in the colors of the Italian flag approached their table and took their order.

Chapter 42

Crackle, crackle, crackle. The stone fireplace was Hayley's absolute favorite part of her dream house. Antonio was at a PTA meeting and she'd just gotten the boys to sleep. When the baby starting crawling she'd have to cover the hearth with a quilt like she did when Tony was a baby so he wouldn't get hurt. The heat warmed her cheeks and hands while her thoughts turned icy. If Antonio went to jail she'd be here alone with the kids. Maybe that wasn't so bad. She wouldn't have to put up with his cheating anymore. It was so embarrassing going into school or even the grocery store knowing everyone she passed pegged her as a naïve fool. Hayley pretended she didn't know what Antonio was up to, but she'd known for a long time. She just hadn't yet decided how to handle it. One of Hayley's greatest attributes was her patience. The purse. She imagined it being snuck out to the car during the first half of the show so the Epi-pen wouldn't be available. Everyone knew how severely allergic Vicky was. Then it was smuggled into their closet. A poor hiding job? Or a cleverly planted piece of false evidence. In a flash of genius she'd thrown away the bag of chopped nuts she used for baking. The police surely would have found it and jumped to conclusions when they searched her pantry. Quick thinking.

***

Antonio was grateful for the solitude even if it meant driving to a boring meeting. His hands were freezing even inside the car. It always took a while for the heat to kick in. He and Hayley hadn't been getting along so well since the police search. It was puzzling that the purse showed up in the closet. The police thought that either he or Hayley—maybe he *and* Hayley—had hidden it there. Obviously, they had no proof since neither one of them was behind bars. When he first met Hayley they had such a connection. He revealed things about himself that he hadn't ever told anyone. Now he wasn't sure if she trustworthy at all. He was realizing that she had some secrets of her own.

Chapter 43

I need to get Mike to clean the windshield, thought Susan. The glare at night is making it hard to see. Downtown was far brighter than the country roads that dominated Westbrook.

"That movie was hilarious. It's the first time I've laughed in a while," said Carolina.

Susan had taken her to Vinnie's for pizza and then they went to the dollar movie downtown. Midterms were this week and Susan knew Carolina had been stressing out over them. She'd hoped to offer Carolina a brief respite.

"I enjoyed it a lot," said Susan." I had wanted to see it when it first came out but Mike and I never got around to it. The pizza was good too." She'd eaten four slices but it was topped with mushrooms and green peppers so at least it was healthy. She couldn't wait to get home and unbutton her jeans.

"That social worker is really friendly," said Carolina. "I remember meeting her at Mom's funeral." They had run into Jody at Vinnie's. "Her friends seemed nice too. "I'm glad she's fending off the DCF while we look for my aunt. I can't believe I even have to worry about being taken out of my own home. Like I don't have enough to deal with."

Susan parked in front of Carolina's house. "I'll walk you in. The lights are all off so Araceli must already be in bed."

Carolina opened the front door and flicked on the light. "Come in for a cup of coffee." She took Susan's coat and led her into the kitchen. "Brrr, it's freezing in here."

"Okay, but I'll just stay a little while. You have school tomorrow and Mike should be getting back from his poker game soon," said Susan.

Carolina filled the coffee maker with water and scooped coffee into a filter. "Did you just hear a noise?" asked Carolina.

"No, I didn't hear anything." Susan was more determined than ever to find Vicky's murderer. She saw how jumpy Carolina seemed these days. Maybe if the killer was locked up in jail Carolina could rest easier.

"Did I tell you I'm already on page two of the scrapbook I'm making?" Susan tried to sound like that was an accomplishment. She really didn't have the patience for scrap booking. Suddenly, they heard the front door slam shut.

"What's that?" asked Carolina.

"Maybe Araceli went out for a walk," said Susan. She tried to sound reassuring but was starting to feel a bit uneasy—like someone was lurking around outside maybe.

"She never does that," said Carolina. They flew into the living room. The door was closed but no longer locked. Carolina opened the door and turned on the porch light. Although Susan didn't see anyone, she heard the muffled sound of a car starting in the distance.

"Who would have been here?" asked Susan. "Is anything missing?"

Just then Araceli came running out to the front porch. "Que paso? What happened?"

They walked in and out of the bedrooms, checked the den, and made sure the silver was still in the kitchen drawer. Nothing appeared to be missing.

"I'll call Lynette," said Susan. Having a daughter on the police force had proven to be a convenience on more than one occasion. Within half an hour, Lynette was knocking on the door.

"Thanks for coming," said Susan. "I think someone was here in the house. We heard the front door slam closed. It was unlocked but Carolina had locked it when we came in. Then we heard a car start and zoom away. It must have been behind the trees of the neighbor's yard." Susan took Lynette to the window and pointed out a dense row of evergreens that lined the neighbor's driveway and obscured the view.

Lynette wrote down the details. Susan knew Lynette would make an official report when she went to the station in the morning. Susan watched as Lynette took a flashlight from her car and checked out the rest of the house. The storm door on the porch was latched from the inside.

"I guess that wasn't the point of entry," said Lynette. Susan followed her as she walked around the perimeter of the house searching the bushes and shrubs.

"Mom, what are you doing? You can't be following me around. It's dangerous. Go back in the house."

Nothing unusual here anyway, thought Susan. She reentered the living room where Carolina and Araceli were waiting.

"Did you find anything?" asked Carolina.

"Look here," Lynette said. She led them down the hallway. "The bathroom window was open. That's how he got in. I'll get the officers who are on duty tonight over here and have them dust for prints. I'm going to go talk to the neighbors. Maybe they saw something."

Susan watched as Lynette crossed the lawn and went next door. The house appeared dark but she saw Lynette climb onto the front stoop and knock. Susan could hear a dog barking but no one answered the door.

Even if the neighbors were asleep inside, Cujo's barking would have woken them up, thought Susan. She watched as Lynette tried the neighbors on the other side. She saw a middle-aged couple answer the door but couldn't hear what they were saying to Lynette. Susan waited with Carolina until the officers were finished.

"Come and stay with us tonight," offered Susan. "It may not be safe. Araceli should go home also."

"I'll be okay," said Carolina. "The police did a thorough search and I have to get up early and get ready for school."

"Lock the doors and call me if you hear anything else," she said to Carolina. "I'll call you in the morning before you leave for school." Susan gave Carolina a hug and left after she heard the door being locked behind her.

Chapter 44

"Do you want some more coffee, Mom?" asked Hayley. Without waiting for an answer, Hayley went into the kitchen, grabbed the pot and brought it back to the table. She poured herself another cup. "The baby was up three times last night. I think he's teething."

"No, thanks. I think you're right." Her mom took a bite of a homemade banana muffin. "He's drooling a lot. You got your first tooth around his age. Rub some teething gel on his gums or give him a frozen teething ring. Poor baby. How's Antonio doing with his new job?"

"Fine, I guess. We haven't been communicating much these days." Hayley felt her eyes beginning to tear up.

"Is anything wrong? Now that he finally has a respectable position is he screwing it up already? I figured he wouldn't be able to handle it."

"Why are you always so negative about him?" Hayley was beginning to feel anger in the pit of her stomach. "Right from the day you met him you didn't like him. Remember? I brought him home for Thanksgiving and I was so excited for you to meet him. You made that grimace you made right when you first shook his hand."

"I did not. I thought he was perfectly lovely," said her mom.

"Don't lie, Mom. You gave him the third degree during dinner. You asked him what his parents did, why he was studying theater, what his plans were. Then after dinner when you and I were loading the dishwasher you told me I could do better. You hadn't known him more than six hours and you already thought he was a loser."

"I was just looking out for you and I was right, wasn't I? How many years did it take before you could afford this house? How many years were you married to a teacher? Guys that go into teaching are either lazy or not very bright."

"You had to keep pushing me to push him. That's why he felt he needed to cheat on me. He knew he could never live up to my expectations, which is ironic because at first I really didn't care how much money he was going to make or how much status he had. I loved him just as he was. But then, you kept second-guessing me and making me feel like I'd settled for less than I deserved."

"Where's the violin music, Hayley? He cheated on you. See, I was right, wasn't I? You're going to divorce him and clean him out of every penny he has. Dad will get you in touch with a good divorce lawyer. I'm sure Arthur will have a colleague he can suggest. And he will never see his sons again. You have to get full custody."

"No, Mom. He'll pay for this but I will determine how, not you. I loved him—I still do. It's about time I told you to butt out." Hayley folded her arms across her chest.

"Hayley, you really need to move on while you're still young enough to find someone else. My friend Tanya has a son who is a cardiac surgeon. His wife died of cancer last year—so tragic. Anyhow, I know the two of you would get along. That's the kind of husband you deserve." Just then, the baby began to cry over the monitor.

"This discussion is over. You can see yourself out. I have to get the baby."

Chapter 45

Westbrook Elementary was eerily quiet first thing in the morning. *Schools were meant to be full of children,* thought Jody. Many of her teacher friends loved the early morning serenity but Jody thought it was depressing. This morning she and Antonio were meeting with the parents of the school terror. Their little blond dynamo was by far more of a terror than any boy Jody had ever worked with. Her rap sheet included setting a fire in the girls' bathroom, throwing a tray of food at the cafeteria manager, and bullying a myriad of students. Her parents didn't look like the parents of a problem kid. They were both well dressed and articulate. Something must have been going on at home though. This type of extreme behavior had roots.

"Hello, Mr. and Mrs. Vigliotti. Have a seat," said Antonio. The conference room was warm and inviting. The walls were paneled and the carpet was plush. Antonio liked that the chairs were thickly cushioned. Sometimes meetings went on for a long time. Jody shook their hands and had a seat. They'd met before on several occasions.

"As you know," said Antonio, Savannah has a history of disciplinary issues stemming from the day she entered kindergarten. We've suspended her countless times, taken away field trips and parties, and even had her write reflections on her behavior. Nothing seems to be working."

"I know," said Mr. Vigliotti. "We can't control her at home either. I'm so sorry that she's causing such a disruption. We've been to three different therapists and they couldn't give us answers."

"Sometimes kids act out for attention or to express anger," said Jody.

"Yes, believe me we know that. She swears she isn't angry and God knows she gets plenty of attention," said Mrs. Vigliotti.

"We're going to try a new solution," said Mr. Vigliotti. "We've been doing research on the internet and there's a facility not far from here that offers a behavior boot camp. It's an eight week session. We're going to pull Savannah out of school for that amount of time. The boot camp has an academic component and they promise the children will not fall behind academically."

"No." Jody's vehement opposition caused Savannah's parents and Antonio to jump. Jody even surprised herself with the power of her own voice. "You must not do that. They will ruin her." Jody stood up and slapped her hand against the oak table.

"Calm down," said Antonio. "These are her parents and they have obviously researched this a great deal."

"You just don't want to deal with her at home." Jody spit the stinging words out of her mouth. "Do you think they will tame her? Make her into your ideal child? What are you thinking?" She felt her face flush with rage.

"I'm sorry, Mr. and Mrs.Vigliotti. Excuse us a moment." Antonio led Jody out of the conference room.

"What on earth is wrong with you? You can't talk to parents that way. They didn't do anything wrong. They're exploring a possible solution—that's more than most parents around here are willing to do. At least they realize there's an issue and are trying to fix it."

"Those camps are horrible. Haven't you seen those stories about kids who go there and are beaten or made to do hard labor in the heat all day without water. A kid even died at one of those places just last year. You know how passionately I feel about the unjust treatment of children," said Jody. She was practically out of breath by this point.

"These parents have done their research. I know the facility they're talking about and it has a wonderful track record. Over the years we've had a few of our students go there and they came back much better behaved," said Antonio.

"They need to accept who that child is and work with her from a position of love and understanding. Do you know how traumatic it will be for that child to be taken out of her home for eight weeks?" said Jody. She had seen this scenario before and it didn't turn out well.

"It's been traumatic for the adults and students here who Savannah has been impacting these past few years. Setting that fire was the last straw. If she doesn't get aggressive help now she'll wind up in jail. You need to apologize to those parents and just maybe I won't write up a discipline report on you," said Antonio. His stern tone caused Jody to step back.

"I'm sorry. This issue is close to my heart." Jody took a deep breath and walked back into the conference room.

"Mr. and Mrs. Vigliotti, I apologize. I know you're doing what you think is best for Savannah. I should never have reacted that way."

"We understand. We know you care about Savannah just as we do. She will come back here a different person, you'll see," said Mrs. Vigliotti.

"Yes, I'm sure she will," said Jody.

Chapter 46

Jody headed back to her office, still upset about the meeting. She ran into Theresa in the hallway.

"Hey, what's wrong?" said Theresa. She was carrying a stack of papers that Jody assumed she'd just retrieved from her mailbox.

"Oh, I just had an upsetting meeting with Savannah's parents." Everyone in school knew who Savannah was, even those who'd never taught her. "They want to send her to that boot camp outside of town."

"So, maybe that's what she needs. I bet her teacher will be happy to hear that," said Theresa.

"Those places destroy lives. I'd never do that to my child," said Jody.

"There are lots of things we see around here that we'd never do. I guess we both are just going to have perfect children. Can we exchange them if they aren't?" Theresa laughed and Jody couldn't help cracking a smile.

"So, how was your date with Prince Charming last night?" said Jody.

"I don't know. I think I want to break up with him," said Theresa.

"Why? I thought you were really into him," said Jody.

"He's getting more and more possessive. If he texts and I don't answer immediately he has a fit. If he asks me out and I have plans with you or Becky, he pouts and tries to make me feel guilty. That police detective called me to invite me out to dinner the other day while he and I were at dinner and he was furious."

"Why don't you just tell him you need a little breathing room?" suggested Jody.

"We already had that conversation—more than once. I'm going to tell him tonight that I don't want to see him any more. There. I've made up my mind," said Theresa.

"Good luck. Call me afterwards and let me know how it goes." said Jody.

"I will. I might need some ice cream therapy afterwards though," said Theresa.

"I'll bring over the Ben and Jerry's," offered Jody. "Cherry Garcia, or Chunky Monkey?"

"Both," answered Theresa. She glanced down at her watch. "Oh, I better go. The kids will be coming in a minute. Talk to you later."

Jody watched her friend disappear down the hall and then went to her office.

She poured herself a cup of coffee. *It feels like it's at least 3:00,* she thought. She was disappointed when she looked at the clock on her desk and saw that it was barely 12:30. She'd just started listening to her phone messages when she heard a knock. She saw Susan Wiles standing at her doorway.

"Oh, hello, Susan. Come on in. What can I do for you?" *She looks so relaxed*, thought Jody. In fact, every retired teacher whom Jody ever met looked ten years younger than they did while they were teaching. "You look great."

"Thank you," said Susan. "I just wanted to check and make sure you were still keeping the DCF at bay."

"Yes, I told them Carolina had an aunt who was coming from out of state to stay with her but they will certainly be following up. Have you located the aunt yet?"

"No, not yet. The police are still searching," said Susan.

"Well I hope they find her soon for Carolina's sake. I'll call DCF though. I've had plenty of experience with them. Stalling isn't usually the problem. Most often I have to stay on them to take action. I'll walk you out."

Jody and Susan walked into the main office suite. A very handsome man with a dolly full of snacks was signing in. As soon as he was out of earshot, Sandra whistled. "Bye, Macho Man. Come again soon," said Sandra under her breath.

"Macho Man?" said Susan. Jody watched Susan's jaw visibly drop.

"Yes," said Sandra. He used to come around here all the time when Vicky was alive. They spent an awful lot of time in her office with the door closed. He had quite the temper though—Vicky had finally met her match. He and Vicky would get into fights and both of them would be screaming like banshees."

Jody wasn't happy to hear that. She hadn't mentioned to Theresa that David had been seeing Vicky. She figured it was past history. But, in light of what Theresa was saying about how possessive he was and that she planned on breaking up with him, maybe she should know this. She'd have to talk to her during lunch. *Oh no,* she thought. *Theresa's class was on a field trip. It would have to wait.*

Chapter 47

Boy, that was exhausting, thought Theresa. Chaperoning a classroom full of kids at a hands-on science museum was no easy task. She'd think twice next time the idea of a field trip popped into her mind. The bus was the worse part. The stuffy heat along with all the noise made her nauseated. She grabbed her purse and stopped by Jody's office but Jody was in a meeting. She decided to go home and try to take a nap before dealing with David that evening. As soon as she got home, she changed into sweats, turned off her phone, and dove under the covers. When she woke up she realized that David would be there in just a few minutes.

I'd better jump in the shower and get ready, she thought. The Japanese Cherry shower gel revitalized her. She would talk to David over dinner. She had to eat after all and maybe he'd make less of a scene out in public. She turned off the water and dried off with the fluffy bath towel she'd treated herself to during last January's white sale. The doorbell rang. *Here goes nothing*, she thought.

"Bonsoir, mi amour. Are you ready for dinner? I'm starving," said David.

"Yes, I sure am. Let me grab my purse," said Theresa. David helped her into her coat. She locked the door and accompanied him to the car. She remembered how impressed she was the first time she rode in his car. Now the BMW seemed pompous and superficial, just like David.

On the way to the restaurant, Theresa rehearsed the speech she would give David. Her palms were sweating even with her gloves off.

"I made reservations at Benihanas," said David. One of the things that had been getting on Theresa's nerves lately was how David never consulted her or took her preferences into consideration when making dinner plans. It was always about what he wanted. She told him many times that she didn't like to eat red meat but dinner plans more often than not involved a steak house.

"Great," said Theresa. They arrived at the restaurant and were promptly seated. The restaurant was illuminated only by the small oil lamps in the middle of the tables. Theresa was glad they weren't sitting at one of the communal tables where the chef cooked for you and a bunch of strangers. That was always uncomfortable. You didn't know whether or not you were obligated to make small talk or if you could ignore them and focus on the people you came with. Theresa heard knives clanking together and the sizzling of food cooking on the table grills. She smelled grilled steak and even though she was mostly a vegetarian these days, the aroma was none the less enticing. Her stomach growled.

"We'll have the steak teriyaki," said David. He ordered a bottle of wine as well.

Theresa waited until they were just about finished eating when she broached the subject of breaking up. "David, I've enjoyed getting to know you these past months…"

"I've enjoyed spending time with you too, Theresa. I think this relationship has real momentum," said David.

"David, I'm not so sure. Honestly, I don't think this is working out any more."

"What are you talking about?" said David. "We're together every weekend and most days during the week. I know you're in love with me, and I love you too."

"David, it should not surprise you that I'm not happy. We've talked about you giving me some space but it just hasn't happened. I'm feeling smothered and I feel like you're always trying to control me," said Theresa.

"What?" Theresa saw David's dark eyes narrow. "You're kidding me right? We're great together. I did give you space. I'm the best thing that ever happened to you. You know how much time and money I've invested in you? I'm the one who decides when it's over and it's not."

"David, I mean it," said Theresa. A relationship is a two way street. You're a great guy, but this is over. I don't want a relationship with you right now."

David sat back in his chair and took a long, slow breath. Theresa felt a little, what was it…scared?

"Okay then," said David. "If that's how you want it, then that's how it will be." He snapped up the check. Theresa felt like every eye in the restaurant was on them. Silently, David pushed away from the table and they exited the restaurant. He was still enough of a gentleman to open the car door for her. Theresa just wanted to evaporate into the night air. *I'll be home in half an hour and this will all be over,* Theresa told herself. Thoughts of Cherry Garcia danced in her head. She started to cry in spite of herself as David sped out of the parking lot.

"David, I need a tissue," said Theresa.

"There's probably a pack in the glove compartment," answered David. Theresa noticed an iciness in his tone.

Theresa opened the glove compartment. She rummaged around with her hand. She didn't find a tissue but she did find something interesting—an Epi-pen.

"David, why do you have an Epi-pen? I didn't know you had any allergies," asked Theresa.

"I'm deathly allergic to bee stings. I carry it just in case." He continued driving past the exit for Theresa's house.

"Where are you going?" asked Theresa. She was beginning to panic.

"You'll see," snapped David.

"David, take me home right now." Her breathing got quicker and she could feel her heart beating in her chest. "Where are you going?"

David was silent and continued driving for what seemed like an eternity. Theresa couldn't read her watch in the dark and realized that in her haste she'd left her phone on her bed. David abruptly exited the highway, winding and twisting now through the mountains. Theresa thought about opening the door and jumping out of the car but there was nothing but dark woods on either side of the road. They hadn't passed another car since exiting the Thruway. She was definitely in a panic.

"David, come on. Where are we going? I'm sorry, I didn't mean it. You know what, let's continue seeing each other. I didn't realize you were in love with me. Now that I think about it, I'm in love with you too."

David gripped the steering wheel even more tightly and kept driving.

Chapter 47

Jody was anxious to get in touch with Theresa. She had a feeling in the pit of her stomach that something was wrong. Jody called Becky hoping maybe she'd seen Theresa.

"Why on earth isn't she answering her phone? It keeps going to voicemail. She's answered before even when she was out on a date. I'm really worried," said Jody.

"I don't know what to say," said Becky. "Maybe she and David are spending the night at a hotel somewhere and don't want to be disturbed."

"She was going to break up with him. She was convinced that she didn't want to continue seeing him. She should have been home by now." Jody had visions of Theresa lying unconscious. Maybe David lost his temper and struck her with something.

"If you're really worried maybe you should call the police," suggested Becky.

"I think I should. I think actually I'll call Susan Wiles. I have her number. Her daughter is a police detective," said Jody. "I think things will move faster if I call her. The police will say I have no proof that anything is wrong."

"Okay, let me know as soon as you find out something," said Becky.

"I will." Jody hung up the phone and immediately went to her contacts list and called Susan.

"Susan, this is Jody Decker. I'm worried about Theresa. She's out with David tonight. She was going to break up with him and she's not answering her phone. She should have been home already. I have a bad feeling about this."

"Well," said Susan, "I normally would tell you not to worry—that they probably decided not to break up and were out having a good time, but I made a connection earlier today. The secretary, Sandra, said David's nickname was *Macho Man* and that he'd been involved with Vicky. Also, Sandra said that David had argued violently with Vicky on occasion. There's one more thing. There was a threatening text left on Vicky's cell phone before she died. It came from *Macho Man*. I think that man is dangerous. I'll call Lynette right away. Let's meet at my house. I'll text you the address." Susan hung up and entered Lynette's number. Lynette picked up on the second ring.

"Hi, Mom, what's up?" said Lynette.

"Jody Decker just called. She's worried about her friend Theresa who's out on a date with a possible psychopath," said Susan.

"Calm down, I'm sure she's fine. How long has she been missing?

"A couple of hours," answered Susan.

"We don't consider someone missing until it's been at least 24 hours. She's a grown up. I'm sure you're over reacting."

Susan thought Lynette sounded like she'd been dozing on the sofa and she knew how her daughter felt about being woken up from naps.

"I'm sure everything is fine. If she doesn't show up for work tomorrow we will get right on it."

Chapter 48

"Where are we?" demanded Theresa. David had dragged her out of the car and was pushing her toward a small wooden cabin. Once David turned off the car it was pitch black. No moon, no stars, no streetlights. Theresa had an odd thought that this was how it probably looked at the bottom of the ocean. She nearly tripped several times on the way to the door. The wooden door creaked. David pulled a chain in the middle of the ceiling and a single light bulb illuminated the musty room. Thick nails were haphazardly nailed into one wall of the cabin. Theresa's eyes scanned the wall—a rake, a saw, a shovel, thick rope. A fishing pole and a tackle box lay in the middle of the floor. A shot gun was propped against the opposite wall. Theresa noticed a refrigerator—one of those old fashioned ones where the entire door opened with a single metal handle. There was also a double burner on top of a folding table. David pulled a metal folding chair out from the table.

"Sit down. Now," demanded David. He went over to the wall and grabbed the shot gun. Theresa's hands were shaking and sweat dampened her armpits in spite of the cold. She didn't know how she was going to get out of this.

"David, I'm sorry; I was so wrong. I actually love you a lot. We have so much I common—we want the same things in life. You're the most handsome man I've ever seen. Please forgive me. Take me back. Let's go back home and start our lives together. Together forever." Now Theresa's legs were shaking too.

"Well, my darling, that sounds beautiful. You and me forever..." His voice became sing-songy. He kissed her on the forehead. "WHAT KIND OF A FOOL DO YOU THINK I AM, "he screamed in her ear. "You've been watching too many Lifetime movies. It's over." David cocked the handle on the shotgun and aimed it at Theresa's forehead.

Chapter 49

Lynette, Susan, and Jody were racing toward the cabin. Jody had managed to convince Lynette that David was unstable and Theresa was not safe.

"Maybe we should see if they went back to one of their places," said Susan.

Lynette drove by both Theresa's apartment and David's house. Both residences were dark. "No one is home. They must still be out together." She called the station and had one of her colleagues run David's credit card records. She also had them run his name through the police database.

"Looks like they were at Benihanas around eight pm. Maybe they decided to have a romantic evening. Let's drive around the area." They checked a few neighboring hotels but no one had seen them. When they got back into the car, Lynette's phone rang.

"Okay," said Lynette. "Thanks, Ted. That's very helpful." Lynette ended the call and turned to Susan.

"That was one of the officers who were researching David. David's family owns a hunting cabin in the Catskills," said Lynette. "Instinct tells me they're headed there."

"Well, let's get moving," said Susan.

"I'll get going," said Lynette. "You stay put."

"You know that convincing me and Jody to stay home is fruitless and time is of the essence. I know you are going to say this is against your better judgment but save your breath and let's go."

Lynette finally agreed to let them tag along. It was beginning to snow and the windshield wipers struggled to keep up with the flakes.

"Mom, take my phone and read me the directions." Lynette exited the Thruway and followed the serpentine mountain road. When she tried to go faster, she skid and nearly hit a tree. Luckily, she was able to get the SUV back on the road.

Susan thought *snow* tires? I guess if you weren't in what amounted to a police chase they may have helped. It was dark and snowing harder now.

"Mom, what do the directions say next?" asked Lynette.

It was so dark now that Susan could hardly read them. "Go right and follow the road. The cabin should be about half a mile on the right." They drove for a few more minutes. Susan spotted it first.

"There it is, Lynette."

Lynette parked the car. Susan had heard her call for backup but right now it was just the three of them.

"Stay in the car. I mean it. I really mean it," demanded Lynette.

Susan and Jody crouched down in their seats and waited for the police to arrive. Susan opened the car window so that she could hear, and stuck her gloved hand out to brush off the layer of snow so that she could see. She watched as Lynette took her gun from its holster, crept up the path, and gingerly opened the door. Susan heard her yell "Drop it."

Chapter 50

Antonio awoke to the aroma of bacon and blueberry muffins. He took a shower and chose a striped blue dress shirt and a skinny navy tie. On the way downstairs, he popped into Tony's room.

"Wake up, sleepy head. Get up and ready for school." Antonio gently shook Tony.

Antonio went into the kitchen and saw Hayley at the stove cooking bacon. He didn't know why he'd been such a cheating jerk. She looked beautiful, even with no makeup and wearing a terry bathrobe. He thought about the first time he met her. He saw her across the courtyard at the student union building. She was eating lunch on the steps of the pit while studying her notes. Her long daffodil-colored hair attracted him first. It hung over her shoulders as she bent forward to eat. He made his way over to her and said something lame like "Aren't you in my poli-sci class?" Her jade-colored eyes had twinkled when she looked up at him and the rest was, as they say, history.

"Have some bacon while it's hot," said Hayley. Antonio was surprised that Hayley was encouraging him to eat bacon. Maybe she was trying to kill him.

"Thanks." He took a platefull and scooped up some scrambled eggs.

"Do you have a busy day today?" asked Hayley. "Can you drop off Tony and come back home? I need to talk to you."

Antonio grabbed his phone and checked his calendar. "No, nothing scheduled for this morning. I'm sure I can get away for an hour or two." Tony hopped down the steps and into the kitchen.

"Have some eggs and a muffin, Tony. Daddy is going to drop you off today but he'll be at school when it's time to take you home," said Hayley.

Tony finished his breakfast and brushed his teeth.

"Here's your lunch box. Zip up your jacket." Hayley kissed him goodbye. Then she turned to Antonio. "I'll see you in a little while." She kissed him on the cheek. Antonio couldn't remember the last time she did that. He was getting a little nervous.

Chapter 51

After getting Mike off to work, Susan decided to ride down to the station and see what was going on with David's arrest. Theresa had seen an Epi-pen in the glove compartment of David's car and he was obviously a psycho. It was only a matter of time until they could charge him with Vicky's murder. Susan was glad that Carolina and Javier would be able to rest knowing Vicky's murderer had finally been caught. She saw Lynette as soon as she entered the station. Lynette's eyes were underlined with dark circles.

"Hi, sweetheart, did you get any sleep last night?" asked Susan.

"Not a whole lot. Come on in," said Lynette.

Jackson was sitting at a desk. Good thing Susan had eaten breakfast. It would have been hard to handle him on an empty stomach.

"Well, good work Nancy Drew. I heard you helped catch a bad guy last night," said Jackson.

"And I never even went to the police academy," replied Susan. "Where were you last night Jackson? Playing Guitar Hero or searching Craig's List for a girlfriend?"

"All Lynette had to do was call me, but I guess she had it covered," replied Jackson.

Susan followed Lynette into her office. "So we got him right? He's the one who murdered Vicky," said Susan.

"Not exactly," replied Lynette. We charged him with kidnapping and he will definitely see some jail time but he didn't kill Vicky."

"But he was *Macho Man*. He threatened Vicky, and you found the Epi-pen in his car," said Susan.

"We found *an* Epi-pen, not *the* Epi-pen. He was telling the truth about being allergic to bee stings. That was his, not Vicky's. We still haven't found the one from Vicky's desk," said Lynette.

"He still could have killed Vicky," said Susan. She crossed her arms across her chest.

"No, he had an alibi which checked out," replied Lynette. "It wasn't him. Besides, can you picture him baking a peanut infused funfetti cupcake?"

"I guess not. I'm disappointed though. I was hoping we'd have closure for Carolina and Javier."

"We will. We just don't have it yet. We will get the real killer."

"You still need to look into *boy toy*, and I'm suspicious of Blaze Conrad's girlfriend. If she was being abused by Blaze, maybe this was her version of revenge."

"We've got it covered, Mom. Go home and relax," said Lynette.

Susan hugged Lynette goodbye and went back home. Maybe she'd try a little more scrap booking.

Chapter 52

Hayley heard Antonio pull into the driveway. Her heart was racing. This was going to be over—today. She had pulled on some yoga pants and a long sleeved tee. The baby had cooperated and was napping in his crib.

"Hayley, I'm here." Hayley heard the door close. Antonio took off his coat and shoes.

"Let's sit down." Antonio followed her into the living room.

Hayley noticed that little twitch above his left eye. Ever since she'd known him, she noticed that he twitched whenever he was nervous about something.

"We need to talk about some things—get everything out in the open. You know I've known for a while that you cheated on me with Vicky. I understand that you may have been trying to 'sleep your way to the top' and in a strange way I understand that. I put a lot of pressure on you to become a principal and build our dream house."

"I wanted it too," said Antonio. "I love our home and I needed a little push."

"Well, you're going to pay for your sins. This is going to cost you," said Hayley. She reached behind her back, slowly.

Antonio looked extremely uncomfortable. Hayley was enjoying watching him squirm.

"Here you go. This is how you are going to make this up to me," said Hayley.

Antonio took the folder. He was expecting the worst.

"Hayley, what is this? Divorce papers?"

"Look inside," said Hayley.

Antonio looked. "Wow, this sure isn't what I was expecting," said Antonio.

Inside the folder were two tickets.

"These are tickets for a European cruise," said Hayley. "A three week cruise. Yes, you are taking me on the vacation of my life aboard the Queen Mary. It's the largest and most luxurious ship on the sea. We will go this summer. My parents have already agreed to watch the boys. Are you surprised?"

"Surprised is an understatement," said Antonio. "This is wonderful. I never would have expected this." Antonio hugged Hayley.

"This is going to be a new start for us, but it will be an expensive new start. I really am sorry I put so much pressure on you. Not that I'm not angry about what you did. I've been seething over that for a long time now and I need to let it go. I want our boys to grow up in a loving two-parent household. I'm even going to try to do some freelance work from home to help out with the finances."

Antonio began to sob. Hayley had never seen him cry before.

"I love you, Hayley, and I'm so sorry. I'll never do anything like that again," said Antonio. This was not the actor speaking. Hayley knew that these words were coming from his heart.

"I'm not even mad about the purse anymore," said Antonio. "I know you planted it so the police would think I killed Vicky."

"What?" Hayley's tone tuned sharp." I never saw that purse until the police showed it to us. I thought you'd put it there. I couldn't believe you had really killed Vicky but I figured maybe you saw the purse in her office and thought there might be something in there tying you to Vicky. I assumed you smuggled it out to the car during all the commotion."

"No, I didn't. I don't remember seeing it in her office at all. If you didn't do it and I didn't do it, who snuck it into our closet? It had to have happened during the party or we would have seen it."

"I straightened up the closet in preparation for the party and didn't see it then. I figured you snuck it in from the car at some point after that."

"No. Do you know what this means?" said Antonio. "The real killer had to have been here during the party."

Chapter 53

Jackson arrived at the station with a cup of coffee for himself and one for Lynette.

"Thanks, Jackson. That was thoughtful. Starbucks coffee just overshadows our station coffee every time. You know, we need to bring Theresa Rizzo up to date," said Lynette.

"I'll go," said Jackson. "I'll go check on Theresa Rizzo and fill her in on the follow up to David's arrest."

"I thought you might volunteer," said Lynette. "Good luck."

Jackson's palms were sweating as he gripped the steering wheel and drove to Theresa's apartment. *What was it about that girl?* His heart fluttered every time he thought about her. He parked the cruiser and knocked on her door.

"Miss Rizzo, this is Detective Simpson. I just came by to check on you. Are you doing okay?"

"As well as I can I guess. I was never so scared in my life. I really thought I wasn't going to see another day. Thank God your partner arrived just in the nick of time. Please come in. Can I get you some coffee?" said Theresa.

Jackson had already drunk a gallon of coffee but he wasn't going to give up an opportunity to sit down over coffee with Theresa.

"Lynette is wonderful," said Jackson. "And that friend of yours, Jody, she's the one who knew something was wrong and brought it to our attention."

"Yes, thank goodness my judgment is better for friends than it is for dates," said Theresa.

"I can't believe you couldn't snag any guy you wanted," said Jackson. He couldn't believe those words just came out of his mouth.

"You flatter me," said Theresa. "I've had a series of losers, one after the other. David, though—he truly takes the cake. Speaking of cake, did David confess to Vicky's murder?"

"No, I'm afraid the bee allergy was legit and he had a solid alibi for the night of the murder. We've got him on kidnapping, though, and attempted murder," said Jackson.

"Well, at least he'll be locked up for a long time I imagine. I'm going to have a hard time living alone here. I slept with every light on, and my cell phone under my pillow," said Theresa.

"I can stop by and check on you if you'd like," offered Jackson.

"You'd do that? That's very kind," said Theresa.

"No problem. Maybe one night I could even stop by after work and bring some dinner."

"I'd like that," said Theresa. "Thank you, Jackson."

Jackson said goodbye and got back into his car. He had a gut feeling that his life was about to take a wonderful turn.

Chapter 54

Carolina was in her room, trying to finish her term paper on Emily Dickinson. *My eyes are getting tired from staring at this laptop,* thought Carolina. *This editing is driving me crazy.* It was so hard to get the correct number of spaces and remember what needed to be capitalized in the citations and in the reference pages. *Maybe Mrs. W. would like a little editing project,* she thought. *I could certainly pay her.* She picked up her phone.

"Hi, Mrs. W., it's me, Carolina."

"Hi, dear. How are things going?"

"This term paper I'm working on is overwhelming. I just don't have the patience I need to get the references and citations correct. I was wondering if I could hire you to edit it for me?" asked Carolina.

"You know I'd help if I could, but I'm terrible with that stuff too. You need someone who's experienced at that," said Susan.

"Yes, but I don't know where to find someone. I don't want to just go online and pick someone. You never know if they're good or not."

"I'll ask around and get back to you. Have you spoken to your dad?"

"Yes, and he sounds great. He thinks another month or so and then he'll be home. Meanwhile, I wish we could locate my aunt."

"I know. I'm surprised it's been this difficult. I'll keep checking with Lynette. Now, you better get back to your paper. It's getting late," said Susan.

"Thanks, I will." Carolina hung up and went back to her laptop. She thought she heard a sound outside her window. *This is really creepy*, she thought. *They never did find out who was in the house the other night.* She looked outside but nothing looked unusual. *I guess I'm imagining things,* she thought. Still she was glad that Araceli was in the house.

Chapter 55

Susan turned off the light and got under the covers. During her working years this had been her favorite time of the day. Now she didn't get nearly so exhausted but it was still nice to curl up on the flannel sheets with Ludwig and Johann snuggled up on the comforter. She wished Mike were there too, but he was doing something on the computer and probably would not be up for hours. She thought about Carolina's problem with the term paper. *I could call Antonio in the morning,* she thought. Maybe he'll know if any of the teachers at Westbrook might be interested. She slept liked a baby. Again, sans Ambien. In the morning she woke up before Mike and surprised him by making scrambled egg whites and turkey bacon.

"Thanks. This is...well...delicious would be an understatement," said Mike.

"I'm glad you like it. I wanted us to eat together before you left for work. I'll get us some more coffee." While she was in the kitchen, Mike slipped some egg white to Johann who was meowing under the table.

"How's the murder case going?" asked Mike.

"I was sure David was guilty but it turns out he had an alibi. Blaze Conrad was eliminated a while ago because his girlfriend showed up and provided an alibi. I still have my suspicions about the girlfriend though. The police haven't been able to tie Hayley or Antonio to the murder in spite of finding the purse in their closet. They haven't been totally cleared though. Then there's Vicky's mysterious sister."

"The one you found out about during your trip to Florida?" asked Mike.

"Yes. And she has motive. Vicky was suing her for the gem collection her mother Mrs. Bowers left."

"Well, it'll eventually be solved. Someone will mess up or new evidence will show up," said Mike.

"I guess so. I have faith in Lynette, and, though I'd never admit it to his face, Jackson is quite a detective," said Susan.

"It's getting late. I'd better go. Making anything good for dinner tonight?"

"Maybe a tofu and broccoli stir fry," answered Susan.

"I said anything *good*." Mike gave Susan a kiss and left for work. Susan remembered that she was going to try to help Carolina find an editor. She called the school.

"Hello, this is Susan Wiles. I was wondering if I could speak with Mr. Petrocelli."

"Hi, Susan. This is Jody. Antonio is at a meeting and won't be back until this afternoon." Jody often helped in the office when one of the administrators was away.

"Maybe you can help me. I was wondering if you know anyone who's capable of doing a good editing job on a term paper. It's for Carolina Rogers."

"Well, as a matter of fact, my friend Becky sometimes does that kind of work. She's a college professor. You met her at Vinny's the night we ran into you."

"Yes, I remember. If you could give me her number, I'll pass it on to Carolina."

"Sure." Jody gave her the number and went back to work.

Chapter 56

Rebecca couldn't believe the coincidence. She'd moved to Westbrook to find out about Vicky and her family, and now her niece was calling her to do an editing job. This was the perfect opportunity to see what kind of a person Vicky's daughter was. She hoped she wasn't vindictive and self-centered like her mom. *Guess I'll find out soon enough*, she thought. She knocked on Carolina's door.

"Hello, you must be Carolina."

"Yes, come on in. Did you have any trouble finding the house?"

"Not at all. Your directions were right on."

"You're a lifesaver," said Carolina. "This term paper is driving me crazy. We can work at the table." Rebecca followed her into the dining room.

"Can I get you some coffee and a muffin? Araceli baked some this morning. She's the housekeeper but surrogate mother would be a more appropriate title, especially since my mom died." Carolina brought out a platter of pumpkin spice muffins. Then she grabbed her paper from the printer.

"Here it is. I printed out a copy. I think the grammar and spelling are pretty good, but I know I messed up on the spacing," said Carolina.

"I see a few spots where you have extra spaces." Rebecca scanned the paper and focused on the reference list. "You need italics here," she told Carolina. "And it needs to be single spaced here." She pointed to a spot on the page. "The writing looks excellent though. I bet you're a good student."

"I try. I'm taking four Advanced Placement classes this year."

"So you're planning on going to college?" asked Rebecca.

"Of course I am. I'd love to get into one of the Ivy Leagues. That's why I'm studying all the time," said Carolina.

"What do you want to major in?" asked Rebecca.

"I'm good at science—maybe Chemistry or Biology. I want to go to medical school eventually and become a pediatrician. I love kids."

"That's wonderful. E-mail the paper to me also so I can suggest changes and it will be easy for you to edit. Do you know how to use the Track Changes feature?"

"Yes, I think so," said Carolina.

"Here's my email address. It'll take me just a few days," said Rebecca.

"I feel better already." Carolina walked Rebecca out to her car and watched her disappear down the driveway.

She seems lovely, thought Rebecca. *It seems like she has her head on straight.* Rebecca had already checked Carolina's social media sites. No pictures of her drinking or acting foolish at parties. No sleazy outfits. No profanity. She mostly posted about school. Even her taste in music was mainstream, like what you hear on the top forty stations. *I'm feeling more and more sure about this*, she thought.

Chapter 57

Susan had almost forgotten that she'd signed up to volunteer at Westbrook. *Let's see*, she thought, *it's been nearly nine months since I retired. I guess I have had enough of a break from the school scene.* Jody had called her and asked if she'd mind helping out at the Teacher Appreciation Day luncheon. Westbrook always put out a beautiful lunch for the teachers. Last year, they served lasagna, salad, sliced ham, and rolls. And the desserts were to die for—éclairs, puffy and bursting with cream, then topped with chocolate gananche. She salivated just thinking about it. Susan stood in front of her closet. *Should I wear my black skirt and blazer? Maybe my gray dress pants with a silk sweater.* Finally, she chose a casual jersey dress. She loved jersey dresses because they could be dressed up or down, they were comfortable, and most important of all, they didn't need to be ironed. She'd given up ironing a decade ago. *I'd better grab an apron*, she thought. Serving food could get messy. She locked the front door. Her Prius hadn't forgotten the commute it had made so many times before Susan retired. Shortly, she arrived at the school. It felt as though she'd never left.

"Susan, it's so nice to see you here. Are you enjoying retirement?" asked Sandra.

"I am. I've been scrapbooking, cooking, and working out. It's nice to have time to explore hobbies."

"I can't wait," said Sandra. "One more year after this one."

"I came to help out at the teacher appreciation luncheon. Are they setting up yet?"

"I think so. You know the way," said Sandra.

When Susan arrived, the teachers' lounge had already been decorated with hearts and white ribbons. There was a large vase full of red and white carnations in the middle of the table with a handwritten sign inviting the teachers to take one.

"Hey, Jody. What can I do to help?" asked Susan.

"There are trays of enchiladas on a cart in the cafeteria kitchen. Can you go get them? We'll set them up here." There was a long, folding banquet table at one end of the lounge. One of the volunteers whom Susan didn't recognize was busy folding napkins.

"I'll go get some ice," said Susan. There were pitchers of iced tea and bottles of soda already on the table. Miss Hadley came in carrying a large bowl of tortilla chips. Susan wondered if they were baked or fried.

"Hi, Susan. Nice to see you here again," said Miss Hadley.

"It feels good to be back. Even better since I can socialize a bit with my old friends, have some lunch, and then go home. No classes to worry about," said Susan.

"I hear you," said Miss Hadley.

"Susan, can you run back to the cafeteria and get the tray of rice and beans?" asked Jody.

"Sure, I'll be right back." The Mexican food smelled delicious. When she returned, the desserts had been set up and there was a large bowl of salad ready to serve. Something about the bare salad being next to the key lime pie seemed out of whack, but she was sure the teachers would love this feast.

"It's show time," said Jody. She tied on her checkered apron with the dog bone appliqué. Susan thought the apron looked familiar which was odd since it was quite unique. She picked up a serving spoon and stood behind the enchiladas.

Every teacher made a comment as they were served.

"This is so delicious,"

"I'm too full to teach,"

"I'll have to skip dinner."

The teachers enjoyed the midday treat and reluctantly went back to their classrooms. Susan hadn't seen some of them in nearly a year and it was nice to catch up on their lives. Kim was newly engaged, and Cindy was expecting a baby. Pam just found out her son was accepted at Yale. *This is the part of working I miss,* thought Susan. When they'd finished serving, she helped Jody clean up.

"Here, take some key lime pie home for Mike," said Jody. "Oh, and these sugar cookies I made. There are just a few left."

"Did you frost these with funfetti icing? They look so festive," said Susan.

"Oh, at the last minute I decided to use up the can of frosting that had been sitting in my fridge," said Jody.

"He'll love these." Susan wrapped up the cookies and pie and headed home.

"On second thought, I have a whole pie here. I think I'll stop by the station and give Lynette a piece. It's on the way."

When Susan got outside, she noticed that it was beginning to snow. She was ready for it to be spring. She turned on the car radio and learned that a blizzard was brewing. *I guess before I see Lynette I'd better stop at Shop Rite and get some extra water and batteries,* she thought.

Susan drove a few minutes out of the way and pulled into the parking lot of Shop Rite. She had to circle the lot three times before finding a parking space. Inside, the store was wall-to-wall people. Susan thought that these shoppers should have known enough to already be prepared. After all, this was New York and it was winter. Then it dawned on her that she was here amongst them.

The store had already sold out of C batteries and only a few cases of bottled water remained on the shelves. She threw a loaf of bread, a few cans of tuna, spaghetti, and a box of graham crackers into her basket. At the last second, she threw in a package of Oreos. The checkout lines were insane. It took twenty minutes to get up to the register. When she came out of the store, she realized that it was snowing harder.

Susan hated driving in the snow. It took her twice as long as usual to get from the store to the police station. When she finally got to the station, Lynette was on the phone.

"Hi, Jackson." Susan wondered if she should be nice and offer him a slice too. "Jackson, would you like a slice of key lime pie?" asked Susan.

Jackson looked surprised at the offer.

"Sure, thank you. I love key lime pie," he replied.

"The roads are getting bad," said Susan.

"I heard this is supposed to be a pretty bad storm. You be careful driving home," said Jackson.

Lynette hung up the phone and approached them.

"You're never going to believe this," said Lynette. "That was the head custodian at Westbrook. He was clearing snow away from the drains out in the parking lot in anticipation of this blizzard they are predicting. Guess what he found?"

"What?" said Jackson and Susan in unison.

"Vicky's Epi-pen from her office. It was still in the original prescription box with her name on it. It was wrapped inside of a plastic bag, so just maybe we have a chance of getting some fingerprints."

Chapter 58

Carolina walked into her kitchen. She still expected to see her mom in there cutting up salad vegetables or stirring sauce on the stove. She wondered if that would ever stop. She couldn't believe they still hadn't found her Mom's killer.

"I bought some canned foods and extra batteries," said Araceli. "Also, more Cheerios and shelf stable soy milk. We probably won't get the blizzard. You know they always hype up these storms and most of the time, thankfully, they never come. Anyway, we're prepared."

"Thanks, Araceli. Becky is coming by in a little while with my paper. She finished it more quickly than I expected. I can't wait to turn it in and have it off of my mind."

"I'll be upstairs watching TV if you need me." Araceli carried a basket of clean laundry upstairs with her. Carolina sat at the table and began texting her friends. Then she plugged her phone into the charger so it would be fully charged in the event they lost electricity. She couldn't imagine what people did during electrical outages before the days of cell phones. At least she'd be able to stay in touch with her friends, listen to music, and play games if the electricity went out. A short time later Becky arrived.

"It's starting to look bad out there. I wanted to get this to you now in case the roads get impassable. It's a hard copy in case you can't access your computer during the storm," said Becky.

"Thank you. I'm excited to see it," said Carolina. She and Becky sat down at the dining room table. While Carolina was reading the paper, the lights blinked on and off. "Oh no, I hope the electric holds up." Carolina continued reading. "Not again." This time the electric stayed off. She could barely see.

"I'll go get the flashlight from the toolbox," said Becky. She groped her way to the sliding door and started to open it. She realized her mistake immediately.

"How would you know about the flashlight, or the toolbox?" asked Carolina. Her fight or flight hormones were kicking in. She started to bolt for the door but Becky grabbed her arm.

"It's not what you think," said Becky.

"Let me go. I'm calling the police right now." Carolina felt around for her phone, then remembered it was on the charger.

"Carolina, no. You don't understand," said Becky.

"I understand. You're the one who's been snooping around my house these past few weeks. What do you want anyway? We don't keep cash in the house."

"Carolina, I'm your Aunt Becky."

"What?" Carolina was completely puzzled.

"I'm your mom's younger sister. Your mom and I were in the middle of a horrible feud over our mom's, actually your Grandma Rosie's, gem collection. She was suing me and I was suing her back but I couldn't stand the relationship being so strained. I moved here at the end of last summer and tried to patch things up with Vicky, but she refused to see me. Then I thought, maybe I'll just give her half of the collection but I knew our mom must have had a good reason for keeping it from Vicky. I decided to find out what my big sister was really like. I hate to admit it, but I spied on her, followed her to see what kind of life she led."

"Did you kill my mom?" asked Carolina. Her hands were sweating.

"Of course not. I was as surprised as anyone when she wound up dead. Someone must have been very angry at her. I wondered what evil Vicky had done and I wondered if you were following in her footsteps. That's when I decided to follow you and see what you were all about."

"So it was you who snooped around the house. You were inside the house the night I came in with Mrs. W."

"Yes, I'm sorry I scared you," said Becky. "I was too embarrassed to face you that night. You do need to make sure you latch that storm door out on the porch and lock your windows for heaven's sake."

"We've been looking for you and here you were right under our noses," said Carolina. "We were trying to find a relative to come stay here until my Dad got out of rehab. The Department of Children and Families was threatening to put me in a temporary foster home."

"I'm so sorry. If I'd known I would have come forward. There was an email from someone claiming to be a police officer but I assumed it was a prank."

"Well, you're here now." Carolina's pulse was just about back to normal.

"Of course, I'll stay here while your dad is gone. I want to have a relationship with you and your dad. I also came to a big decision."

"What kind of decision?" asked Carolina.

"I sold the gem collection for a lot of money. I kept a few special ones. I had a sapphire necklace made for you. It's your birthstone, right?"

"Yes. Thank you," said Carolina.

"I've already set up a college fund for you and I had my financial advisor invest the rest of your share in a trust fund that you can access after you turn 21."

"Are you kidding?" said Carolina.

"It was the right thing to do. You're a good person, Carolina, and you have some wonderful goals in life. More importantly, we're family. You're my only niece. If Grandma Rosie had known that she would have done the same. She just didn't trust Vicky with money."

"I can't believe this. I'm so glad you're here," said Carolina.

"Me too," replied Becky.

Chapter 59

It was a good night for scrapbooking, thought Susan. Mike was working late and the snow falling outside made the house seem extra cozy. Susan pulled out the envelope of pictures she'd snuck out of Carolina's house. She had gotten a brilliant idea. She would make a scrapbook of Vicky's life for Carolina. She had recent pictures of Vicky from school and Carolina had practically handed these to her on a silver platter the day she went over to her house to look for clues. She cut the border of a snapshot with her funny jagged scissors and glued it onto the scrapbook page, then searched for her next addition.

Here's the one of Vicky's best friend and her son, she thought. Something bothered her about that picture. What was it? Suddenly the apron with the dog bone appliqué screamed at her from the photo. Now she remembered why Jody's apron looked familiar. She wondered how it was possible that Kara and Jody would have the same quirky apron. Then she focused on the boy in the picture. He would have been around Jody's age. Jody did come from upstate. Maybe she and the boy had been friends or maybe they'd gone to school together. The boy was strange looking, kind of like a tortured soul. Jody seemed to gravitate toward those kinds of kids. She was always trying to help them. She peeked outside. It wasn't snowing all that hard. Curiosity got the better of her. She tried calling Jody but it went to voice mail. *I'll just have to drop by her apartment,* she decided. She'd gone over there to return the pie dish and it wasn't very far.

There had to be a logical explanation. Kara and Vicky had been living in the same town after college according to Carolina. She pulled on her boots and scraped the snow off the windshield of her car. *Oh my God,* thought Susan. Maybe that boy was *baby boy* from Vicky's contact list. What if Jody found out that her friend was being abused by Vicky. *I know Jody would have tried to intervene,* thought Susan. It was snowing a bit harder now but Jody didn't live far. Susan had to drive slowly but she made it safely to Jody's apartment. She knocked on Jody's door.

"Susan, I'm surprised to see you here." Jody was wearing well-worn sweats and had her hair pulled into a ponytail.

"I tried to call but your phone went to voicemail," said Susan.

"I must have forgotten to turn the sound back on. Come sit down. What can I do for you?" asked Jody.

"I know this seems silly and that I must have too much time on my hands, but remember the apron you were wearing for the teacher appreciation luncheon?"

"Yes. What about it?" said Jody.

"It's so unusual. I mean, I've never been in a store and seen an apron with a dog bone appliqué. It looks like it was hand sewn."

"And…what is it you want to ask? It belongs to my mom. She left it when she came to visit last month," said Jody.

"Your mom lives in Ithaca, right?" asked Susan.

"Yes. What does that have to do with anything?"

"Well," said Susan. "I was at Carolina's one day and we were looking at photos of her mom. I took some of them to turn into a scrapbook for her. Anyhow, there was a photo of her mom's best friend Kara. Kara was wearing that apron. I noticed because I'd seen an episode of the *Martha Stewart Show* where they showed how to personalize clothing with appliqué. I was exploring sewing as a hobby but even with my bifocals it was impossible to thread a needle. Caused more stress than it was worth. I just couldn't figure out why you had the apron. Did you know Kara? You both lived in Ithaca and you had the exact same apron." Right on cue the power flickered and the house became dark.

"Here. I'll light these candles," said Jody. "No, I never knew anyone named Kara."

"Are you sure? Did your Mom know her?" asked Susan.

"I said no. Can I get you some hot chocolate? You must have been freezing outside."

"That would be nice," said Susan.

"Good thing I have a gas stove," said Jody. She grabbed a flashlight from the kitchen drawer.

"Are you sure you didn't know Kara? Something about that apron keeps nagging at me," said Susan.

"Why do you keep pushing me on this? It's just an apron. It's just a coincidence. Here, have some hot chocolate." Jody handed the mug to Susan. Susan noted a hint of annoyance in Jody's voice. The ring tone of her phone startled both of them. Susan saw that it was Lynette and figured it might be important.

"Hi, honey. Um, yes that's right. I'm all snuggled up at home just working on my scrapbook. It's nice of you to check up on me. Yes, Dad's still at work. Are you home? What? You found a match to the prints on the Epi-pen? Whose prints are they? Do they belong to someone we know? Okay, finish up and get yourself home. I'll call you later."

"Was that your daughter?" asked Jody.

"Yes. Great news. They found a match to the prints on the Epi-pen they found in the parking lot. My daughter and her partner are on their way to make an arrest."

"That's great," said Jody. Did she tell you who the murderer is?"

"No. Lynette can be a stickler for rules. She can't tell me anything until after they make the arrest. There was a young boy in the photo," said Susan. Maybe you knew him?"

"I told you to let it go," said Jody." I'm beginning to lose patience. Maybe you should leave before the storm gets worse."

"It's weird," continued Susan, without missing a beat. "A dog bone appliqué. It couldn't be a coincidence. You have to have some connection with Vicky's friend Kara. Maybe you knew the boy in the picture."

"I said DROP IT." Jody's voice was loud and abrasive.

Susan had never heard Jody speak in the tone of voice she was using. Now Susan was confused. Something strange was going on here.

"You did know him, didn't you?" said Susan.

"Leave this alone. You're butting into something that doesn't involve you," said Jody. Susan detected sweat on Jody's brow. She couldn't imagine why since it was freezing in the house. Susan noticed that Jody was breathing harder now too.

"I'm thinking that maybe you two were friends. Maybe you were trying to protect the boy. Were you protecting him from Vicky? Was she doing things with him that she shouldn't have been doing?" asked Susan. Suddenly Jody grabbed her car keys and bolted out the door to the driveway. Susan followed closely behind her.

"Damn," said Jody. "You parked behind me. Move your car right now!"

Susan was sure that she was close to getting the truth out of Jody. Otherwise, why would Jody go off the deep end like this?

"Jody, calm down. Tell me what happened. Were you trying to protect your friend from Vicky? Did you hurt Vicky? I know how crazy you get when you think a child's in harm's way."

"Give me your keys right now," said Jody.

"No." said Susan. "You can't drive in this state of mind and the roads are slippery to boot. Let's talk about this."

Jody grabbed Susan and reached into Susan's pocket for her keys. Susan held on with a death grip. Jody was undoing Susan's grip, finger by finger but before she could get possession of the keys, Susan flung them across the yard. She guessed those tricep exercises must really be working because she threw them far enough that they couldn't be found under the swiftly falling snow.

"Why did you do that? Now we're both trapped here," said Jody. She reluctantly went back into the house. Susan followed.

"You knew him, right?" said Susan. You somehow wound up in the same school as Vicky all these years later and you killed her to protect your friend. That's why you had left over funfetti frosting to use on those sugar cookies. It was left over from the poison cupcake you made for Vicky. Was Vicky still harassing your friend? Was he the one who Vicky listed as *baby boy* on her contact list? Lynette's on her way. You might as well get the story off your chest."

"*Knew him?*" said Jody. "I *was* him. It should never have been a boy in that picture. It should have been a girl. It was a girl, only packaged in a boy's body."

Susan was really confused now. Jody's eyes pierced the dark room.

"I told my mom I was a girl. I knew all my life. She tried to force me to do boy things like football and skateboarding. She didn't know what to do with me. When I put on one of her dresses one day and said I was going to wear it to school, she flipped out and called her best friend—Vicky Rogers. She trusted Vicky. Vicky was a teacher back then. She was around kids all the time and she had a degree in education. Mom trusted her. After my dad died, she went to Vicky all the time for advice. She asked Vicky what she should do about me."

"And what did Vicky tell her?" asked Susan.

"She told her about this camp she knew about. It was a place where they changed behaviors. The church ran it. Mom assumed I was gay. She had no understanding whatsoever about what it meant to be transgender. Truthfully, I wasn't sure what it meant either. I only began to understand myself years later."

"What happened at the camp?" asked Susan.

"Well, first of all they preached the bible day and night. They told me I was going to go to hell if I didn't change my behavior. Then they tried to 'pray away the gay.' We would meet in a group outside in a huge tent. There was fire inside—lots of burning coals. It felt like a sauna. It must have been 120 degrees in there. They would pray over us for hours and hours. We weren't allowed to eat or drink. The tent door was zipped and one of the counselors stood guard. I was terrified that it would catch on fire. It's a miracle it didn't. A few of the children passed out from the heat."

"Oh, Jody, that must have been horrible," said Susan.

"It was. They berated us, even physically beat us. I couldn't believe my mom had put me in such a place. I called her one night. I had to sneak out and use the payphone at the gas station down the road. I begged her to come get me. She said she would but she didn't. I called her back the following night. She said she'd called Vicky and Vicky told her it was for my own good—that she had no choice but to leave me there so I could heal."

"You must have hated your mom and Vicky too," said Susan. "I don't blame you."

"The word *hate* is such an understatement. I vowed I'd get revenge, even if it took the rest of my life," said Jody.

"Then you killed Vicky?" asked Susan.

"After I got out of the camp, I went into a severe depression. I even tried to commit suicide but my mom found me before it was too late and called an ambulance. They pumped my stomach at the hospital. It was touch and go for a few days but I survived. They transferred me to the psychiatric ward and diagnosed me with bipolar disorder. Mom was elated that the doctors had figured out my problem. That's all she wanted, was a nice simple explanation for my behavior. She thought that was the end of my insisting I was really a girl trapped in a boy's body."

"You must have been so confused and upset."

"I had a very long road ahead of me. First, they had to keep adjusting the meds. One day I couldn't get out of bed. They adjusted my dose and then I couldn't get to sleep. I lost weight because I couldn't eat, then I gained weight when they changed to a different pill. The worst thing was that the real problem was being buried. I still couldn't make anyone understand that I really wasn't a boy. Vicky was right there at my mother's side telling her how I just needed to stop trying to get attention."

"I'm so sorry, Jody."

"The minute I turned 18, I left home for good. I didn't speak to my mother for many years after that. I was on a roller coaster throughout my teen years. I can't believe I actually graduated high school on time and with a scholarship to boot. Oh, I wasn't headed for Harvard or anything. It was a scholarship to attend community college but I saw it as a chance to break free. I knew I wanted to find a career in which I could help people—specifically children. "

"And you did just that. You've helped so many children just in this short time you've been at Westbrook. And you were even helping Carolina even though she is Vicky's daughter. That wasn't in your job description," said Susan.

"I can't resist helping a child in need. It's not Carolina's fault that her mom was a good for nothing bitch. Anyhow, to continue my story, while I was in college I found a support group for gay, lesbian, and transgender students. Seeing that announcement on the library bulletin board saved my life. I understood for the first time that there was nothing wrong with me. I got the support I needed to learn to love myself and to take steps toward leading the life I was meant to live."

"Did you get back in touch with your mother? I understand support groups often help repair families," said Susan.

"I wrote her a long letter explaining the process I was going through. Vicky was still interfering, I knew. Eventually Mom did accept me as a daughter. We've been redefining our relationship these past few years. She even said she was proud of me for going into social work. That I didn't expect," said Jody.

"So what happened with Vicky? Did you get your revenge?" asked Susan.

"Oh yes. I plotted my course very carefully and patiently. I knew she'd become principal of Westbrook.

For several years I kept my eye on the job openings there and last year—*Bingo*. I applied for the social worker position and I got it. Even the job description mentioned that Westbrook was a peanut-free magnet school. A peanut-free magnet school? How crazy was that? When I interviewed for the position, Vicky explained that she herself was deathly allergic to peanuts. I filed that piece of information away."

"Are you saying it was you who killed her?" asked Susan.

"That woman was dangerous. She nearly ruined my life and then she was even recommending behavior boot camps to some parents at our school. She had to be stopped," said Jody.

"What did you do?" Susan swallowed hard. She was having a difficult time digesting all of this information.

"I didn't have the guts to just walk up to Vicky with a gun and shoot her, not that I own a gun. I'm not a violent person. When the PTA announced the bake sale they were doing during the holiday concert, the idea came to me. I would bake a cupcake especially for Vicky. She would assume it was from the bake sale and therefore hypoallergenic."

"So you made a poison cupcake?" Susan asked. She was perspiring despite the freezing, dark room. Was she in danger? If Jody had killed Vicky, she could just as well kill her. She wished Lynette were there.

"It wasn't exactly a poison cupcake—only if you happened to be allergic to peanuts. I just crushed some peanuts in the blender and threw them into the cupcake batter. Added some almond milk too. I made a happy little cupcake just for her. I decorated it with lots of frosting and sprinkles on top. Then I put it on her desk during the first half of the show, knowing she'd probably go to her office during intermission. I was right."

"Jody, that's murder," said Susan.

"I prefer to think of it as paying a consequence. It was a stroke of luck that her angry husband came in and punched her. They didn't even put together the cause of death for weeks. The world is a better place without Vicky Rogers in it."

"How did Vicky's purse get in Antonio's closet?" asked Susan.

"I took it off Vicky's desk when I brought the cupcake. I knew she carried an Epi-pen with her always. Then I remembered she kept one in her drawer as well, so I took that too. I rushed out to my car and stashed the purse in my trunk. I must have dropped the other Epi-pen on the way to my car. The night of Antonio's party, I took it with me inside my super-sized purse. I went upstairs to use the bathroom and planted it in the closet. I figured that would slow the police down for a while."

"Jody, we have to call the police. You took Carolina's mother away from her."

"Believe me, she didn't need a mother like that. I've saved her years of therapy," said Jody."

"That's not for you to judge. If you explain that you were a victim throughout your childhood or even that you've been diagnosed with bipolar disorder, maybe the court will go easier on you," suggested Susan.

"No, Susan. That isn't going to happen. You need to keep this between us."

"I can't. I understand how you felt, I really do, but that doesn't justify murder."

In the candle-lit room, Susan saw Jody enter the kitchen. She heard Jody rummaging through drawers. Susan knew this was her chance to escape. She grabbed her keys from her purse and tiptoed to the front door.

"Oh, no, you don't," said Jody. "You aren't going anywhere." Jody took a heavy wooden rolling pin from behind her back and raised it above Susan's head. Susan ducked just in time. Didn't Jody just say she wasn't a violent person? Susan was contemplating her next move when the front door burst open.

"Police! Drop the weapon." Lynette and Jackson were there, guns out. Jackson put handcuffs on Jody.

"You're under arrest for the murder of Vicky Rogers. You have the right to remain silent..." Lynette finished reading Jody her rights.

"Lynette, how did you know I was here? How did you know Jody was the murderer?" asked Susan. Her heart was still beating in overdrive.

"Shortly after you left the station, we got a hit on the prints that were on the Epi-pen that the custodian found in the parking lot. We ran them through the database and they matched Jody's. It's a good thing we require fingerprinting for school employees or we never would have made the connection," said Lynette. "What on earth were you doing here anyway?"

"Well, I just got a confession," said Susan. You were going to be my first call."

"Had you lived, that is," said Lynette. That rolling pin could have done some real damage. What do I tell you all the time about snooping?"

"I'm sorry, Lynette. At least we solved the case. I can't wait to tell Carolina and Javier. I still can't believe it was Jody who did this."

"You never know what people are capable of given the right circumstances," said Lynette. "Let's go. We'll drive you home. Dad can bring you back to pick up the car tomorrow when the roads are clear."

Jackson walked over to them. "Are you sure you're okay?" he asked.

"I'm fine, thanks to my daughter and her fearless partner." *Maybe Jackson wasn't all that bad*, thought Susan. It was snowing so hard that they could barely see the police car. Lynette and Jackson dropped Susan off at home on the way to the station.

"Wow, what a night. I can't wait to get home and crawl under the covers. The snow's really coming down now," said Lynette.

"Go ahead and get some sleep," said Jackson. "I have one stop to make first."

Chapter 60

Jackson got into his car and headed toward Theresa's apartment. He'd been stopping by every day on his way home from work to check on her. He had no doubt that one day they'd get married and start a family. She was so warm and so funny. Smart too. When he got to her street, all the lights were out. He parked in her driveway, made his way up the icy sidewalk to her door, and knocked.

"Jacky, I'm so glad to see you." Theresa greeted him with a huge bear hug. The electricity was out and judging by the freezing temperature inside of the apartment, he figured it had been out for a while.

"Are you okay? I was worried about you being alone during the storm," said Jackson.

"I'm better now that you're here," said Theresa. "I'll admit it was creepy sitting alone here in the dark."

"Theresa, I have some terrible news about your friend Jody."

"What? Is she alright? Did she get into an accident?" asked Theresa.

"No," said Jackson. "Jody had problems that she kept very well hidden."

"What problems? She'd have told me. I'm her best friend," insisted Theresa.

"I don't know how to tell you this. Jody was just arrested for Vicky's murder."

"What? No, I don't believe it, not for a second." Theresa looked completely confused. "Why would Jody kill Vicky?"

"Jody has had a tough life. She realized early on that she was transgender, though she didn't have a label for it. Her mom thought she was gay, which she isn't. She identifies with the female gender although physically she was born a male," explained Jackson.

"I still don't understand how that's related to Vicky's murder. This is totally crazy. Jody's one of the girliest girls I know. She loves clothes and makeup. This must be a mistake."

"Jody had planned to kill Vicky for quite some time. Her mother was Vicky's best friend. Vicky encouraged her friend Kara to send Jody to a behavior change program. It nearly killed Jody. She blamed Vicky for the trauma she underwent and for destroying her relationship with her mother."

"Poor Jody. I had no idea. This is hard to digest," said Theresa.

"Jody will stand trial but hopefully she'll also get the help she needs," said Jackson.

"And you know what, Jacky? I'll still be there for her. It's horrible that she was compelled to commit a murder, but I can't imagine how much pain she must have been in to drive her to that point."

"You're a good friend, Theresa. I knew you were special the minute I met you," said Jackson.

"Jody always helped people. She gave all those wacky kids at school the benefit of the doubt. She always tried to see things from their perspective," said Theresa.

Jackson couldn't help himself. He embraced Theresa and gave her a long, slow kiss.

"I took out a bunch of blankets," said Theresa. "We could cuddle up on the couch, to stay warm."

"Yes," replied Jackson. "To stay warm. Sounds like a plan." He took off his shoes and cuddled next to her.

There was nowhere in the world he would have rather been.

"You know Jacky, the roads are awfully treacherous. It may be better not to chance driving. Maybe you should stay here tonight." said Theresa.

"I thought you'd never ask," said Jackson.

Chapter 61

Carolina felt like a kid on Christmas morning. Her dad was being released today. Although it had been nearly a month since Jody was arrested, she still couldn't believe that the sweet social worker turned out to be a murderer. Carolina hoped that Jody would spend the rest of her life staring at the walls of her jail cell. She hoped Jody would feel lonely and scared every single day. Although she was glad that her mother's killer was paying the consequences of her actions, it didn't make Carolina miss her mother any less. *At least I connected with my aunt Becky,* thought Carolina. Carolina had been spending a lot of time with Becky lately. She respected her and enjoyed her company. It was remarkable that Aunt Becky had voluntarily decided to share the inheritance with her. She could have kept it all. *I never would have known about it,* thought Carolina. At least she didn't have to worry about paying for college now. Becky sent a text telling Carolina that she was out front. Carolina opened the front door and decided to swap her coat for a sweater. The sun was out, the snow had melted, and the bareness of winter was evolving into the abundance of spring. It felt like a new beginning.

"Hop in," said Becky.

"Hi, Aunt Becky. I can't wait to pick up my Dad. I'll ride home with him if you don't mind, but remember we're going out to dinner tonight to celebrate."

"Wouldn't miss it for the world. I know your dad was assigned a sponsor but you and I will need to support him too. We need to make sure he goes to his AA meetings. Also, I got in touch with Human Resources at Ohio State. They want to interview your dad for a job doing technical support. He can work from home. With the new push for virtual classes, there's a big need for 24 hour tech support," said Becky.

"Aunt Becky, you're amazing. Thank you. I know he was worried about finding another job," said Carolina.

"I'd do anything for my favorite niece. The three of us are family now." Becky twisted and turned the steering wheel en route to Coventry.

Carolina noticed buds on the previously bare trees that were interspersed between the evergreens. Anticipation made the ride seem interminable. It was like waiting to open Christmas presents. Carolina remembered how when she was younger it used to seem like December was the longest month of the year. She and her mom would open the little doors on the advent calendar every night but it seemed as if the days were passing in slow motion.

Finally, Becky announced, "Here we are." She pulled into a parking space and turned off the key. Carolina practically ran to the elevator. Javier was dressed and waiting in his room with several suitcases. The rest were still in the trunk of his car.

"*Mi hija*, I'm so glad to see you. You too, Becky." Javier hugged them both.

"I can't wait to have you back home," said Carolina. They walked to the elevator and then out to the parking lot where they found Javier's car. Carolina slid into the passenger seat.

"Oh, no, *hija*." Javier tossed the keys to Carolina. "You've been sitting on that learner's permit for months now. It's about time you learned how to drive."

Chapter 62

Birthdays sure go by faster the older you get, thought Susan. What a year it's been. Last year at her birthday dinner she had to worry about getting home early enough to prepare for work the next day. *No worries this year,* she thought.

Susan made a wish and blew out the 61 candles on top of the cream cheese frosted carrot cake. Dozens of balloons were taped to the wall of Lynette and Jason's dining room. Colorful streamers hung from the chandelier. Mike took out his camera.

"I was thinking about funfetti but decided against it," said Lynette. She put her arm around Susan and gave her a hug. Then she cut the cake and began serving it. Jason took the Moose Tracks ice cream out of the freezer. It was Susan's favorite.

"This is divine," said Susan. "Since it's my birthday, calories don't count, right? I'll have another piece with extra ice cream."

"Well, this has been quite a year," said Mike. "I think you've found new hobby—solving mysteries."

"Please don't encourage her," said Lynette. After they finished their cake, Lynette said, "Come on, let's open presents." They went into the living room.

"This one's from me," said Mike. Susan tore open the paper and opened the black velvet box. Inside was a Pandora bracelet. "Oh, my God, this is beautiful," she said. She gave Mike a kiss.

"Look at the charms. The first is a heart. Self explanatory. And the other one is a spyglass," said Mike.

"I love it," said Susan.

"Here's one from us," said Lynette. She handed Susan a shirt box wrapped in pastel birthday paper. "Open it."

Susan tore open the paper. She never was one of those people who opened the paper delicately and folded it to reuse. She opened the box, which Lynette had taped shut, and pushed aside the tissue paper. "Oh, my God!" She lifted the t-shirt out of the box. It said: *World's Best Grandma.*

"Is this for real? Are you going to have a baby?" asked Susan.

"Yes, Mom. You and Dad are going to be grandparents."

"This must be what an out of body experience feels like," said Susan. She hugged Lynette and Jason.

"And you're going to be a grandpa," said Lynette to Mike.

"I'm the happiest man in the world right now." Mike hugged his daughter.

"No, I think I'm the happiest," said Jason.

Susan had a feeling that this was going to be a fantastic year.

The End

About the Author

 Diane Weiner is a mother of four and a veteran public school teacher with a broad range of teaching experience. She has previously published several music education articles as well as a doctoral dissertation but finds writing fiction to be much more fun. Westbrook, NY, the fictional setting of the Susan Wiles School House mysteries, bears remarkable similarities to the small town in upstate New York where Diane grew up. She currently resides in South Florida with her husband of many years, their youngest daughter, two cats, and a bisch-a-poo. When not writing, Diane enjoys long distance running and spending time with her family.

www.ingramcontent.com/pod-product-compliance
Lightning Source LLC
Chambersburg PA
CBHW020321260626
47156CB00004B/1326